Dreamweaver

Lauren Hallstrom

Printed in the United States of America.

ISBN 978-1-937862-51-0
Library of Congress Number 2013917415

Published by BookCrafters, Parker, Colorado.
BookCrafters@comcast.net
http://bookcrafters.net

Cover design by Shantana Judkins
and Susan O'Brien.

Copies of this book may be ordered from
www.bookcrafters.net
and other online bookstores.

*To my family,
who said they knew it
all along.*

Prologue

The citizens of Fortune had always been superstitious. It was how they'd been raised from childhood, something they grew up believing and never stopped. Ever since Roger Garrison had found a stray penny lying in the place that was now the town square, the citizens had looked for luck all around them and clung to it. That penny had been facing heads up, which was a sign of good luck. Roger Garrison had gone on to found a small town there, and he named it Fortune because, as he said, someone could always find luck there, whether it be good or bad. Not long after, he became extremely wealthy and spent the rest of his life traveling the world.

For this reason, the citizens embraced every sign of good luck, hoping for the good fortune that penny had bestowed upon their founder, and they looked for every opportunity to pass it on. Maybe that explained the knowing smiles on several peoples' faces when the old man entered the grocery store.

The old man was smiling as well. His eyes crinkled and each wrinkle, each small crease on his face became more pronounced and more visible than before. He didn't mind.

He stood near the entrance of the supermarket and watched the shoppers pushing carts past displays of precariously stacked pyramids of canned goods and cereal boxes. They all seemed to be in a hurry, as if they'd rather be anywhere than in a store that smelled of freshly baked bread. He shook his head in dismay.

The man watched as a little boy and girl ran in circles around the cart their mother was pushing. The mother looked annoyed, but the man was delighted. It was good to see children. This was just the chance he had been waiting for.

The boy skidded around the cart once more and grabbed the rim for balance. He pushed his feet off the ground and jumped into the basket of the cart. This startled his mother, who stopped with her hand to her heart. The girl watched her brother from outside the cart. "No fair!" she cried, "I want to ride in the cart too!"

The mother threw up her hands in exasperation. "Thomas, after five minutes you need to get out. Then it will be Molly's turn." She resumed pushing the cart. The old man imagined the cart wasn't as easy to handle now that there was an energetic young boy inside.

The man stepped out of the corner and rummaged around in the pocket of his brown jacket. From it he produced a shiny penny. It glistened and gleamed under the harsh light of the supermarket.

The man slowly walked forward and placed the penny on the floor in the middle of the aisle. He was careful to place it heads up. That was important. He backed away to watch what followed.

Molly, Thomas, and their mother headed directly toward the spot where the penny lay. No one had noticed it yet. Suddenly, Molly squealed and raced toward the penny. She picked it up in her small hands and lunged at her mother to show her. "Look, Mommy, a lucky penny!"

At this, a smile lit the man's face. *Children are very clever*, he thought to himself.

"That's nice, honey," her mother answered absentmindedly, checking the price of bananas. "You can put it in your piggy bank."

The old man turned away, satisfied. That little girl would have a good day. A very, very good day.

As he left the store, the man heard Molly ask, "Can we go buy a trampoline, Mommy?"

This time her mother looked straight at her. "You know, that's the funniest thing. I was just thinking about that. I think we can arrange for an early Christmas present for you two."

The little girl's huge eyes said it all.

Chapter One

"I look like a Christmas elf," I moaned as I stared at myself in the mirror. I loved green, and I loved the emerald knee-length dress I was wearing. But with a mane of dark red and a sprinkling of freckles, I looked more like a holiday commercial than a fifteen-year-old girl going to a party.

"Oh, come on," my mother said lightheartedly, "This way you can wear it again when we go visit the relatives at Christmas!"

"Mom!" I shrieked, and burst into laughter, with Mom joining in. After a moment, I gasped for breath and started hiccupping, which just made me laugh harder.

Finally we both managed to calm down. "What do you say we head out now, Audrey?" Mom asked me. "We'd better or we'll be late."

I sighed and nodded my assent. My gaze returned to the mirror once more. At least my hair was smooth and relatively straight, but it was a deep, dark red that stood out from my super pale skin. If you looked, you could even see small yellowish hairs intermixed with the red ones. I used to joke that while most people's hair turned gray as they aged, mine would be completely blond by age thirty.

I reached out to steady myself as I stood. I was wearing high heels, and I hadn't quite gotten used to them yet. Before I got to the door I grabbed the black sweater hanging from a hook on the wall. It was a good thing too, for as soon as Mom opened the front door a chilly breath of air accosted me. It was only September, but it already felt like winter.

Mom followed me out and gave an inadvertent shudder. "Let's hurry," she urged. "It's cold enough already."

The fall party was held each year in the town's school gym. We lived in such a small town that driving really wasn't necessary—everything was within walking distance. Still, I didn't enjoy the walk into town when it was as chilly as it had been lately. Since we lived on the outskirts of town, it was a longer walk than I would have liked.

Thankfully, it wasn't too long before a large brick building came into view. It was a building I knew well as I had gone to school there for the past ten years.

Across the double door entrance hung a bright orange banner that read: *Town of Fortune Annual Fall Celebration* in big letters. Everyone in Fortune was welcome, and it certainly looked like the entire town had come.

Mom squeezed through the entrance and wove through the crowd inside while I followed close behind. People shot looks of annoyance over their shoulders, but when they saw who it was their faces relaxed and they smiled. Mom was well known in town for her kindness and sweet disposition. She was the one person who was always willing to help when a neighbor lost a dog or the school needed a volunteer for a special event, and so she had earned many favors over the years.

"Why, Pheraby Waverly, how very good it is to see you!" A high, gracious voice interrupted my thoughts. I looked up and immediately recognized the town gossip, Mrs. Tweedy. Fortune wasn't so small that everyone really knew everyone, but I did know quite a few people.

Mom recognized her too. Mrs. Tweedy made her way daintily through the crowd and stopped in front of us. Mom clenched her teeth and tried to smile politely. "Hello, Mrs. Tweedy." Mom abhorred her first name Pheraby, and went by her middle name Elaine. Mrs. Tweedy paid no mind to that though, and was the only person in town to call Mom Pheraby. Personally, I loved the old-fashioned Southern name that had been passed down for generations in her family. Besides, I thought Pheraby was a prettier name than Elaine, but I kept my mouth shut.

While Mrs. Tweedy chatted with Mom about how expensive cantaloupe had become, I busied myself with looking around at the other people already here. I recognized Mrs. Jenkins from the grocery store and several classmates in the crowd.

Mrs. Tweedy now turned her attention to me. "Why, Audrey, honey, look how much you've grown!" she exclaimed giddily, patting me on the head. "Before you know it she'll have herself a young fellow," she proclaimed to my mother.

I felt my face flush bright red. I'm sure it was a

wonderful combination with my hair. Mom smiled at me sympathetically, but Mrs. Tweedy didn't notice my discomfort and kept talking. "Oh, and you two simply *cannot* forget to take a fortune cookie!" She gestured at a bowl off to the side of the room. "I got one already. It said I'm going to find myself a penny richer in the near future! That's always a good thing, isn't it?" I gave her a big fake smile, hoping I could slip away when she wasn't paying attention. No such luck.

Mrs. Tweedy herded me and Mom over to the fortune cookie table. It wasn't really a Chinese-themed party, but Fortune's fortune cookies were a tradition for almost every party or get-together. I didn't mind them, but Mom thought they were pointless and silly. "Why don't you go ahead and have one, Audrey," Mom suggested. She added, "I'm not that hungry right now. Maybe I'll have one later."

I knew she wouldn't, but I didn't say anything. I grabbed a cookie from the bowl and broke it open after glancing up at Mrs. Tweedy, who had her hands clasped together in anticipation. I extricated the small slip of paper from the cookie and turned it over. The tiny, perfectly shaped words were printed in red.

Your choices will decide the fate of those around you.

Well, that was ominous. An unexpected shiver ran up my spine. "What does it say?" Mrs. Tweedy wanted to know, leaning forward.

I looked up at her with feigned nonchalance. "Oh, the usual. It's ridiculous." I was relieved when Mom suggested we get some punch, and we said goodbye to a disappointed Mrs. Tweedy.

I led the way to the punch table. This building served as the school for every age group in Fortune. With students from ages five to seventeen, it was a very crowded place, especially during a party.

As I neared the punch table someone bumped against me and I stumbled. I fell headlong into the table in front of me. Mom caught my arm just before I dunked my head into the punchbowl, but the damage was already done. Several students snickered. At least they had the decency to hide it behind their hands.

I straightened carefully and summoned all of my dignity. I plastered an amused smile on my face and took a deep breath.

"Do you want to go home?" Mom whispered.

Almost imperceptibly, I shook my head. I wouldn't give them the satisfaction.

✳✳✳

Our house looked different at night. In the daylight it was cheerful and greeted people with its pretty shade of yellow paint, a white picket fence, and lovely little flower gardens against the house. But returning in the dark after the party, the house appeared to be masked in shadows. It was a hulking dark figure amidst a sea of long, drying grass.

We went inside and Mom cheerfully suggested a salad for both of us. I smiled at her gratefully and agreed. My good mood had returned. I was never upset for very long. I didn't need to be. Besides, where did being upset ever get me?

I watched Mom run a hand through her dark, choppy hair and then rip pieces of lettuce with her nimble fingers. She never minded cooking or preparing food. In fact, she loved it. Cooking was soothing and methodical for her. Somehow I always managed to dump half of the milk on the floor or burn the toast for breakfast. That's why Mom didn't ask me to help and I didn't offer.

While I waited, I wandered into my room. Our house was a one-floor cottage. It was a little cramped, but that's how I liked it.

My room was located directly across from Mom's and next to the bathroom. I flopped down onto my turquoise beanbag chair next to my stereo. Out my picture window that made up nearly an entire wall in my bedroom, I could just make out the tall grass in the distance, swaying in a light breeze.

Absentmindedly, I picked up a miniature snow globe. I shook it and watched the snow flutter down and finally settle over the tiny features and carvings of the town of Fortune inside. My father had given it to me years ago. I still remembered that day well.

✱✱✱

It had started as a normal day like any other, but it ended perfectly. I had the week off from school and I was spending it playing board games with Mom, mostly *Candyland*. I loved that game. I had made a new rule that the winner got to eat a handful of Skittles from a bowl we kept on the counter. We had played five games, and I'd already eaten four handfuls of the candy. When we finished the sixth game, Mom asked me, "What should we play now?"

"*Candyland!*" I screeched gleefully.

"Again?"

"Yes!"

Suddenly I heard a door slam and a deep voice call out, "I'm home!"

"Daddy!" I yelled and ran to him, my bare feet padding against the hardwood floor.

"Whoa, now!" he called, laughing and spinning me around in a circle. Then he set me down. "I have a little something for you."

My eyes sparkled and I grinned up at him. "What is it?"

Dad carefully pulled something out from his coat pocket. The tissue paper crinkled as he removed it from the gift and tossed the paper aside.

It sparkled in the light and I gasped. It was a snow globe. I shut one eye and peeked in the glass to get a better look. Many houses were lined up one by one on either side of a street. I saw shops and restaurants with names too tiny to see. And off on one side was a little meadow with snow-covered grass and a little yellow house.

"It's Fortune, isn't it Daddy?" I asked with delight.

"It sure is," Dad laughed. "Now, whenever you want, you can watch it snow over the town of Fortune."

I lunged forward and wrapped him in a huge bear hug. He scooped me up and set the snow globe on the hall table. "How about we go outside and play for a while?" he suggested.

I rode piggyback to the backyard. We had a large oak tree with a swing that hung from the thickest branch. Dad put me on the wooden seat and began to push me higher and higher. I giggled and held tight to the ropes on either side, tilting my head up and staring as the huge expanse of never-ending sky came closer. I closed my eyes and reached out, imagining my fingers were brushing the clouds. I was a bird, and Dad was my wings.

***

I sighed and blinked my eyes several times. Without realizing it, I had started to cry. It wasn't a particularly sad memory; in fact, it was my best one. My perfect day. Wistfully, I looked out the window again and closed my eyes.

Chapter Two

I must have fallen asleep. Soft morning sunshine streamed in from my window and I stretched, awkwardly getting up from the floor. My muscles were extremely sore and tight, which made me regret sleeping half on a beanbag chair and half on a rug for twelve hours.

Suddenly a giant white fur ball landed on my head. "Rice Krispies, Shelby!" I hollered, "Give me a little warning before you do that!" My cat meowed at me as if to say, "I didn't do anything," and commenced licking her paw.

Then I realized where she had jumped from. Papers and books from my desk were strewn across the floor and a cup full of pens had fallen over. "Bad cat," I scolded Shelby, petting her at the same time. She looked at me warily for a moment but then relaxed, apparently deciding I was not much of a threat.

***

I walked into the kitchen ten minutes later and found Mom waiting for me. "Good morning, sleepyhead," she teased.

I knew that I hadn't returned to the kitchen for salad last night and hastened to explain. "Sorry, Mom, I didn't mean to—"

She cut me off, telling me it was fine. "More Bacon Bits for my salad that way!"

At the table, I chugged down a glass of orange juice and inhaled a bagel. Mom eyed me and laughed. "Hey, what's the hurry?"

I swallowed a mouthful of bagel. "I'm going out hiking."

"Okay, just don't forget your coat. It's chilly."

As I grabbed my coat from the hook, I happened to glance at myself in the mirror mounted on the wall. Two large eyes stared back at me—one green and one chocolate brown. No one else I know has two different colored eyes. I guess I'm just different. People call me quirky, and I suppose I am. But when I stand waist-deep in tall grass as far as the eye can see, or next to a river that roars so loudly it obscures my thoughts, it doesn't matter. Nature doesn't care what I look like.

I left the house, letting the back door swing shut behind me, and trudged through the grass and crunchy leaves on the ground. I had no idea where I was going—my feet seemed to take over, as usual.

As I walked, the landscape turned from flat, empty fields to slight hills and denser patches of trees. I was heading away from town toward the wilderness beyond.

I felt dampness in the air and thought that it might rain—or snow. It certainly was cold enough for it.

When I finally reached my unconscious destination, I parted the branches of the trees and entered the clearing. I smiled at the familiarity of it all. This was where I went whenever I needed to listen to silence for a while. Not complete silence, for the sounds of the rustling of leaves and the birds leaving their nests for the winter were present.

I cleared away some of the fallen leaves from the ground and found the circles of mushrooms on the forest floor. They were called fairy rings. I didn't believe in magic, but this clearing was a powerful place to me. I picked a few blue wildflowers and put them in my hair. Sitting down on a log, I sighed in contentment. To me, this place was perfect—fungus and all.

In the trees further on, I knew there was a little stream with large rocks along both sides. I could hear the gurgling and rushing of the water even now. I didn't usually go that far into the forest, though. To get to the stream I had to climb over the rocks along its banks. I didn't like the thought of standing up so high with nothing but shallow water to break my fall.

I glanced at my watch and did a double take. More time had passed than I thought. A beautiful place can do that to you.

I hurried my pace on the way home but I hadn't gone even halfway before it began to snow. I didn't mind, though. I turned my face to the sky and tasted the snowflakes on my tongue. They melted immediately, and I laughed. Webs of snow crystals formed on my hair, and flakes coated my eyelashes. It was more often cold than not in Fortune, but it never snowed enough for me. The snow picked up fast, and soon it covered every surface with a thin layer. If I didn't get back soon, Mom would be worried.

Eventually, I arrived home. No one was upset that I was late—not even Shelby, although she did give my snow-covered shoes a curious look.

***

The old man walked along the path that was blanketed with fallen leaves. The snow had mostly melted, but it had moistened the leaves, turning the red- and yellow-speckled things into a soggy mess.

A cool breeze blew across his weathered face and caressed the folds of his large jacket. One penny remained in the shadowy confines of the coat pocket, waiting to see the brilliant light of day.

All the rest had found themselves on the wooden floor of the old dance studio or on the empty seat of the merry-go-round. Those pennies had surely changed lives.

The lone penny shifted inside the pocket, awaiting the call of the old man.

Surrounding trees watched his progress along the path, and the atmosphere was heavy and ominous. The old man did not notice. The shadows grew and lengthened as the sun lowered itself over the mountains and the area went quiet.

He wasn't aware when the penny slipped out of his pocket and hit the ground with a *ping!* He didn't notice it roll along the slabs of stone on the edge of the dirt pathway.

The penny hit a crack in the stone and came to an abrupt stop. The tails side faced up. The man had no idea, and the sense of foreboding that arose in the air did not warn him of what was to come.

Chapter Three

Gravel crunched under my feet, and I was once again hiking. Two chipmunks ran across my path, chasing each other and making me laugh. The sun warmed my face, which was rare for a September morning in Fortune. Everything was perfect.

I didn't know how wrong I was.

The snow had nearly cleared already thanks to the intense sunlight, so my eyes caught the gleam of something lying on the edge of the path to town. As I got closer, I could make it out. It was a shiny new penny with that never-been-used-before look, just lying there in a pile of rotting leaves.

Most people would not even bother to stoop down to pick up a penny. It wasn't worth it to them. But if you've learned anything about me so far, it's that I'm not like most people. My green and brown eyes and obsession for chocolate fudge brownie ice cream were enough to tell that.

So, I stopped and reached down. My fingernails brushed against a particularly slimy brown leaf, and

I shuddered, but I picked up the penny anyway and stashed it in my wallet, which I returned to my back pocket.

A twig snapped and something rustled behind me. My breath caught as I spun around, eyes wide. I would just about die of embarrassment if a little bunny popped out from the brush.

Nothing happened. I let out my breath a little and called, "Is someone there?" My voice quavered just a little bit.

No answer. Not even a little bunny rabbit showed itself. I turned away, feeling silly. Everything was fine, right? After all, it was broad daylight. What was I expecting? Drama was reserved solely for Hollywood. And people like Mrs. Tweedy, who lived for it.

As I started back home, all thoughts of my little adventure faded away. I was anticipating a little snack of chocolate fudge brownie ice cream. That would just about make my day.

***

Back home, I entered the kitchen to find that it was surprisingly dark. "Oh good, you're back," Mom said in greeting.

"What happened? Why is it so dark?" I was confused. I looked over my shoulder. The hallway light was working just fine.

I could tell Mom was a little perplexed too. "I don't know. One minute the light was working fine, and the next you came in and it just flickered and went out." She shrugged. "A couple of bulbs must have gone out." She opened the curtains on the window over the sink to let in more light and returned to her task of peeling carrots from the vegetable garden.

It must have been a coincidence. I leaned over the countertop covered with dirty dishes and recipes clipped from magazines, and I flicked the light switch a couple of times. Nothing.

"Would you mind helping me with this stew I'm making?" Mom looked over at me when she saw me still standing there biting my lip. "All you need to do is slice these carrots for me. I think even you can manage that." She winked at me.

I moved over next to her and reluctantly took the knife she held out to me. The blade gleamed in the light from the window and I winced. I disliked everything about knives, even the kitchen ones. The pointed tips, the serrated edges—they scared me. But I wasn't willing to admit that. It seemed kind of childish. I just hoped fervently that I wouldn't cut myself or send the carrot (or the knife) flying through the air.

I started slowly but soon got into a nice rhythm of *chop, slide, chop, slide.*

Hey, maybe this isn't so bad, I dared to think. Suddenly, the knife slipped on the surface of the carrot and fell against my left hand, slicing the skin on my index finger. I dropped the carrot, which rolled, discarded, on the floor into a corner, and I cried out in pain. Mom rushed over as I clutched at my finger, biting my lip so hard I thought it might be bleeding too.

"There now," Mom said, keeping up a constant stream of low, comforting words that probably calmed her more than they did me.

She helped me treat the wound and wrap it in a small bandage. "It's not so bad that it needs stitches," she reassured me.

Thank goodness. "Now, why don't you go to

your room and rest for a bit. I'll take care of the rest of this." Mom gestured toward the mess of carrots and other vegetables on the countertop. I nodded numbly and headed to my room—so much for my ice cream snack. In my room I had plenty of time to think about today's unfortunate events.

But what *had* happened today? I struggled to understand. Maybe it was nothing, but it sure didn't seem like it. I had worried about cutting myself before I began to chop the carrots. Was this regrettable event due to a failure of concentration or something more? My head hurt just trying to process it all. Maybe I was just thinking too much.

I sat down by my window and stared out at the scarecrow in the vegetable garden. I had made it myself to, naturally, scare away crows. Right now it wasn't working. A crow perched on the scarecrow's shoulder and seemed to stare straight at the house—straight at me. I squinted at it. The bird was not intimidated in the least. If anything, the scarecrow looked more scared than the crow did. I looked away and the crow flew off in a flurry of black feathers and flapping wings. Things just kept on getting more and more interesting.

Chapter Four

Viktor Sharpe sensed the presence of the darkness the second it broke through its chains. He looked up, hesitating. Could it be? It had been nearly twenty years since the last time—but no—he felt it in his very bones. After all, he was well acquainted with darkness. He could not be wrong.

Sharpe grinned devilishly and arose, his black cloak swirling about his ankles. It was close. He let the darkness guide him. He sensed it was only a small bit condensed in one tiny mass, but that was no matter, he told himself. Somewhere in the back of his mind he wondered how it had been summoned. He had tried countless times in the past decades but had not been able to bring it forth. It had been locked in a place that was unreachable—until now.

It wasn't long before Sharpe reached the forest. It was broad daylight, but the trees were so dense that he would have no trouble concealing himself if he needed to.

Something made him slow down. Branches

overhead swatted at him and numerous thorns sought to draw blood, but Sharpe deflected them all as easily as if they didn't exist. He stared ahead, intent only on one thing.

Ah. He smirked in satisfaction and at the same time raised a thin eyebrow. It was a penny. Such a simple thing. How interesting—such trivial things shouldn't contain such power. As Sharpe watched, a young lady appeared on the dirt path. Her hair floated in the wind and she was almost skipping, clearly happy. Sharpe thought she looked ridiculous. After making sure he was completely concealed, he settled back to watch the event unfold.

It took an eternity for the girl to notice the penny, and even longer for her to finally decide to pick it up. Sharpe grew impatient and he struggled to contain his frustration.

When the girl finally took it, he narrowed his eyes. Though she probably hadn't noticed, he certainly did—it would have been impossible for him to miss it. As soon as her fingers came in contact with the coin, the darkness inside of it burst into life, shimmering and undulating. It was similar to a combination of fire and murky water.

Sharpe had never seen the darkness behave this way before. It had taken on alarming characteristics that darkness should not have. This wasn't right. In a moment of distraction he stepped back, accidentally snapping a small twig on the forest floor.

The girl's head shot up immediately. Sharpe was amused. They always seemed to scare so easily. He stilled and did not move, and was surprised how easy it was considering how many years had passed without practice.

She stared straight at him but did not see him

through the thick foliage. Her eyes startled him. Sharpe crept closer, even though he already knew there was no need. Her eyes were two different colors—one green, one brown. Sharpe had never expected to see eyes like that again, but he was wrong. She was one of them.

A sense of wariness warned him to get away, but he stayed. She was so much more powerful than she knew.

The girl mumbled something about bunnies. Sharpe scoffed to himself, *if she only knew...* He brought his attention back to his original intent. How was he going to get that coin? The girl had put it in her pocket. He could always simply grab her and take it by force. He would have felt completely comfortable with that before he saw what she was, but now he wasn't so sure.

Suddenly he had an idea so brilliant he swelled with pride that he had thought of it. He would let her keep it. With her power, it might just be enough to do the job.

A slow smile spread across his face as he wrapped himself in shadows and vanished undetected.

Chapter Five

The dream accosted me as soon as my head hit the pillow.

I was indoors in my own house, but it was different. All the lights were out, and I couldn't see a thing. No matter how hard I tried, I could not find the light switch.

Suddenly I heard a soft voice whisper, "Audrey..."

I found myself outside, standing in dead grass. It was a strange shade of yellow-brown, and it reminded me of thin, wriggling worms. I noticed then that I was standing dangerously near the edge of a steep drop-off — a cliff. Before I could move away, I saw an eerily familiar figure. I called out, "Dad?"

He raised his head, and I saw that it was him. I made an unintelligible sound of astonishment and raced toward him. "Dad, are you okay? How did you get — "

As I reached him, I noticed his features were

strangely distorted. A horrible grin spread across his face. It was then that I realized it was not Dad, but a huge crow that transformed in an explosion of black feathers that slowly floated to the ground. The rocks underneath my feet crumbled, and I screamed a silent, yet piercing scream. I felt nothing as I fell, but on the point of impact I jerked awake.

My back arched and I could almost feel my body hitting the ground in my dream. I lurched and lost my balance, almost crashing to the floor.

As I caught my breath, I noticed my door was cracked slightly open. Had Mom seen me writhing under my blankets? Shelby came up to my face and meowed inquiringly. "It's okay, Shelby," I assured her. "It was only a nightmare." A very strange one. I sat up completely, and Shelby immediately walked over my legs and stood on top of my pillow. She lay down, tucked in her chin, curled her tail around one paw and fell fast asleep. "Silly cat," I laughed. She certainly didn't seem worried about bad dreams.

***

Later that day, I was debating whether to go out to buy chocolate fudge brownie ice cream (it turned out we didn't have any left in the freezer) when Mom called out to me from the kitchen, "Audrey, we're out of sugar and eggs and I'm going to need some for the brownies I'm making. Do you think you could run out to the store and get them for me?"

Sugar! Energy! It made me giddy just thinking about it. "Of course I'll go," I said. There could never be too much sugar in the world.

Mom handed me a twenty-dollar bill and told me she expected the change back. "Don't forget the eggs!" she called out, laughing as I ran out the back door. *Eggs? What eggs?*

It didn't take long to get to the supermarket as it was in the part of town we were nearest to. I quickly grabbed a bag of sugar and even remembered to get the eggs. Then I happened to notice a sale on candy. A display of Skittles raised my excitement greatly. Why not get a package of Skittles too? I added one to my shopping basket.

At checkout, I glanced at the other people in line. They all looked familiar, but I knew none of them well. "Hello, Audrey," a man in a dark overcoat greeted me. I looked up at his obscured face but couldn't place who he was, even though he looked familiar.

"Hi," I replied after an awkward pause.

When I finished my purchase, I wandered out of the grocery store. It was built on the only large hill in town. There was one road which sloped up to the top. It wasn't a particularly long road, but it felt like it whenever I climbed up to buy groceries. I never looked forward to that part of the walk, but I didn't mind the walk back down. When I was little I used to lug a wooden sled all the way up and sled down the middle of the street. It was the only place we kids deemed appropriate for sledding. I smiled at the memory.

On another side of the store the ground dropped off sharply several hundred feet from the bright red front doors. Today I felt a strange urge to go over to the cliff. I tentatively walked over and looked around. My eyes widened. Strange. It reminded me a bit of my nightmare last night.

A flash of black whipped across my peripheral vision and I stumbled as I glanced over my shoulder. All I noticed were a few people looking at me strangely. I didn't blame them. I took a step back, but my foot came into contact with only empty air. I gasped, managing to hang on to the handles of the grocery bag with one hand. Time seemed to slow enough that true panic set in. One thought penetrated my mind: *Just like my dream.*

A firm hand grabbed my flailing arm and pulled me up easily to safe ground that *didn't* crumble. I fought the urge to get as far away as possible from the drop-off.

"That would have been a nasty fall," the owner of the hand observed, peering over the edge of the cliff.

"Th-thank you," I stuttered, brushing the dirt off my jeans. I checked the eggs to make sure they hadn't broken.

"Don't mention it." The speaker was a boy about my age. He grinned lopsidedly. "Seriously — don't. Enough people are staring at us already."

I turned. He was right. I even thought I saw Mrs. Tweedy pulling out her phone, probably to inform someone of the latest gossip. I could just imagine her saying, "I'm telling you, that Audrey Waverly just stumbled over her own feet and almost fell straight off the overhang by the grocery store! Yes, I'm sure…"

The boy cleared his throat uncomfortably, and I shook the disturbing thoughts away. "Um, thanks again for saving me." My voice was pitched unusually high. "I'm Audrey. Audrey Waverly."

"I know," he said with an easy smile. "I've seen you around town."

Really? I squinted at him, trying to remember if I knew him at all. Was he in my class?

"I'm Jonathan Lake," he continued. "I just moved here, so you probably don't recognize me."

I decided I didn't. I was surprised, though. Usually a new family was front-page news in Fortune, but I hadn't heard anything about anyone moving in.

Jonathan ran a hand through his streaked light brown hair. "Well, I hope to see you around — hopefully under better circumstances," he gestured pointedly in the direction of the cliff.

I smiled sheepishly. "See you."

I began to head down the hill toward home. As I walked down Main Street, I passed rows of houses painted varying shades of brown. They all looked the same. I could never understand why anyone would choose to live smack in the middle of a city, even a tiny one like Fortune.

When I turned off Main Street, a pretty little plaza in the middle of a tiny shopping center came into sight. Stone paths trailed through the area and large flower pots sat scattered across the plaza. This was where the town hall stood, towering over all the surrounding buildings. It was a beautiful building with wooden carvings over the entrance and smooth, cylindrical pillars in the front. But what I liked best was the huge water fountain that stood in front of the shops. It was the pride of Fortune — imported from France and paid for by the wealthy Roger Garrison, the founder of the town.

The fountain was a pure white that shone even brighter in the sunlight and was illuminated by moonlight during the night. Designs of swirls and curlicues were carved onto the sides. In the center a rearing horse stood pawing at the air. Some people said it had once been a unicorn but townspeople had thought it foolish and broke off the horn.

The fountain ran during all hours of the day for much of the year. The water spurted out over the horse and rained down the sides into the bottom of the fountain, only to be brought back up again.

And under the water at the bottom lay thousands upon thousands of coins—mostly pennies, but others too. I even saw a soggy lump of a dollar bill half-floating near the edge.

As I approached the fountain an aging man looked up at me and smiled. I didn't recognize him. "Hello. Audrey, isn't it?" he inquired.

"Yes, that's me," I confirmed. Why was it that everyone knew me, but I didn't know them? I had lived in this town all my life, after all. Didn't that count for something?

He was sitting on the edge of the fountain and he patted the spot next to him, gesturing for me to sit down. He treated me like an old friend. I hoped I wasn't losing my memory.

I obliged his unspoken request and sat next to him. After a moment, I finally gathered the courage to ask him his name.

"I'm sorry, sir," I apologized, "but I don't believe we've met before. Who are you?" I cringed as soon as the words left my mouth, realizing how rude they sounded.

The man only chuckled. "Oh, I apologize. Please excuse my manners. I'm afraid I'm a bit rusty at introductions." He paused a moment, as if trying to remember the proper way to continue. "My name is Carson Gray. Feel free to call me Carson."

"All right, Mr.—I mean Carson." It felt strange calling a man at least sixty years my senior by his first name.

When I looked over at him, I noticed that he was cocking his head and peering at me oddly, furrowing his brow in thought. I started to ask him if something was the matter, but he spoke first. "You are special, Audrey Waverly," he told me, enunciating each word clearly. I was silent. I didn't remember telling him my last name. He continued, "I can feel that much about you. Don't you ever think otherwise—you are anything but normal." He leaned back, satisfied for a moment with what he had told me. Then he gave me an amiable, almost fatherly, smile.

"If ever you would like me to tell you more, you can find me here," Carson told me. "Always here."

Chapter Six

The words of Carson Gray, the man I had met by the fountain, continued to play over and over in my mind the next day. *You are special, Audrey Waverly. You are anything but normal.* I knew I wasn't normal, but still, did he know something I didn't?

I found Mom in the computer room at her old desk. She had a pair of bright purple reading glasses perched on the end of her nose. In her hands was a slip of paper—a slightly crumpled receipt. She turned when she heard me come in. "I notice you bought a *'Skittles Megapack'* on that trip to the store," she commented, glancing up at me over her glasses.

I grinned sheepishly, idly wondering where I had put that bag of candy.

Mom raised her eyebrows at me and consulted the receipt again. "I fully expect you to pay me back for that. It was $2.01, after tax."

I sighed and retrieved a handful of crumpled dollar bills from the pocket of my faded jeans. I handed Mom two of them and she looked at me expectantly. "Wait a sec," I told her. "I know I have some change around here somewhere." I fished out my wallet and looked through all of the little pockets. In the last one lay one penny that gleamed in the light. "Eureka!" I cried, simply to break the silence, and Mom laughed. I handed the penny to her and she flinched when it touched the skin on the palm of her hand.

"Is something wrong, Mom?"

"No, it's nothing." She gave me a shaky smile and slipped the penny into her pocket.

✱✱✱

I decided I needed to see Carson again. I hadn't told my mother about almost falling off a cliff because if I had, I would likely not be going out by myself for quite some time. Still, I felt guilty for keeping something as big as that from her.

The most peculiar thing was how similar that accident was to the nightmare I'd had the night before it happened. I couldn't recall exactly what happened in the dream anymore, but the feeling of it was the same. I dismissed the idea. It was just a strange coincidence, that's all.

I had no idea where Carson lived, so I headed along the path to town, hoping to find him where he said he'd be — by the fountain.

When I reached the familiar area of little shops circling the fountain, I looked around eagerly but did not see him among the few people there. My shoulders slumped. I started to circle the fountain and it was then that I saw him. He sat on the edge on the opposite side of the fountain — the exact same place he had been sitting last time. He noticed me right away. "Ah, Audrey! I had a feeling I might see you again." He smiled warmly and there was just something about his expression that made me relax and let my breath out just a little.

"I assume you have come to hear some sort of explanation from me because you have been confused. Am I right?" His eyes twinkled merrily and he was undoubtedly in a good mood. I wondered how he had gotten so close to the truth.

"Yes…Carson…you said I was unusual." I sat down next to him and he nodded encouragingly. "I was wondering what made you think that." *Please don't let him say something about my eyes.*

"I must say, I do pride myself in being able to see the unusual," Carson said thoughtfully. "I can help you to see your own power and inner strength," he told me, "but first, is there something troubling you?"

I don't know what made me trust Carson. He wasn't much more than a stranger, after all, but I felt like I could tell him anything. I just hoped I wasn't making a mistake. "Well, yes," I stumbled over my own words. "For the past few days I've had several—accidents. Strange things that I thought were just coincidences, but now I don't think they are."

Carson looked concerned. "What kinds of things have happened?"

"Well, yesterday I almost fell off a cliff and two days ago I cut myself badly with a kitchen knife." I bit my lip. "I'm not normally that clumsy, I swear!" To my ears though, I sounded like a sniveling, whining child who was simply overreacting.

Carson seemed to think differently, but then our conversation took an unexpected turn. "Audrey, what frightens you?"

I didn't know what that had to do with anything, but I counted off several things on my fingers, "Heights, spiders, weapons, black licorice…"

Carson smiled at the last item, but I suddenly realized something. "Wait a minute—heights and weapons. In both cases I was afraid of some aspect of the accident: the height of the cliff and the knife itself."

Carson nodded. "Do you know what that means?"

"Um, that I scare too easily and forget to be careful?"

He smiled wryly. "Not exactly. Let's see, I don't know the best way to explain this. Was there something else out of the ordinary that you saw or did that happened around the same time?"

I considered. "There is one thing, but it sounds completely crazy. I did find a penny on the ground before both of those things happened." I laughed inwardly at myself. The words sounded ridiculous.

I thought it was nothing but as I spoke, Carson's cheery smile melted into a frown and he became dead serious. "Which side was facing up?"

His intensity frightened me. "I—I think it was tails."

Realization was plain on his face and he turned grim.

"What is it?"

Carson turned to face me and I noticed his eyes had lost their previous luster. "Tails is more than plain bad luck. You see, a certain evil resides in a penny that drops and lands tails-side up. That evil is released when someone picks it up." His eyes met mine. "The one who possesses that penny is, in a way, slowly tortured by his or her own fears.

When you picked up that penny, Audrey, your very nightmares came to life."

I sat there in shock for a moment, unable to process what Carson had just told me. What if he was just kidding, just messing with me for the fun of it? But, no, what he said made an uncanny kind of sense. It seemed like my nightmares were alive both in my strangely vivid dreams and in life. It had to be true. But that begged the question: how did Carson know?

Before I had the chance to ask him about it, Carson put his hands on my shoulders and faced me. "What happened to that penny?" A certain urgency made his rough voice quiver slightly. When I didn't answer right away, he asked me again. "Audrey, where is the penny?"

I searched my mind, trying to remember what I had done with it. "It's here, in my wallet," I said suddenly, and pulled my wallet from my pocket. I searched through it, but all I could find was my student ID card and the few remaining crumpled dollar bills. Where was it?

Then I remembered. "I gave it to my mom!"

Horror filled both of our faces. "Maybe it won't be so bad," I tried to convince myself. "My nightmares weren't so bad. It's all right." It was my chant, my prayer.

But Carson shook his head. "Nearly plunging to your death isn't so bad? And it only gets worse. The longer someone keeps it, the worse it will get. And if it gets passed on to others, terrible things will happen." He shook his head and his eyes glistened. He whispered something to himself, something I couldn't quite hear clearly. Something like, *"I never meant for this to happen again."*

My panic was real now and I was glad there weren't any shoppers out gawking at us. "What do I do?" I asked Carson somewhat hysterically.

"Go home." Somehow he managed to stay calm while I was a complete wreck. "Find your mother and get the penny back. Give it to me if you can. Neither of you should have it in your possession for long."

I nodded and got to my feet quickly. "Where will you be?"

"Here. Always here."

I thanked him and dashed off, almost crashing into a storekeeper closing his shop, in my haste.

I bolted down the street and onto the dirt path to home, my breath coming in short gasps. Beads of sweat formed on my forehead and I brushed them away angrily. There was definitely no time to rest.

My shoe connected with the tip of a rock that jutted out from the middle of the path, and I fell flat on my face. For a moment all I could see were the individual grains of dirt. Then I was up again, running for my life. Or, rather, for Mom's. My palms stung and ached and I could taste the sharp tang of blood in my mouth.

I tried to ignore it all as I ran, thinking only of Mom, but every sensation was sharper and clearer to me than ever before. I felt my hair whip in the wind and fly in my face. I lost precious seconds while I stopped to push the tangled strands out of my face so I could see where I was going. I was sure I had blood on my face and my hair was a mess, but I didn't care. I just had to get home.

It seemed like eternity before the little yellow cottage came in sight.

I flattened the purple chrysanthemums in the

front as I trampled them and flew up the three steps to the door.

Fortunately the front door was unlocked. I pushed it open so hard it flew back on its hinges and rammed into the wall behind it. "Mom!" I screamed shrilly.

She appeared in the hallway with a dishtowel in her hands, looking frightened. She took in my disheveled appearance and her eyes widened. "Audrey, honey, what's wrong? Are you okay?"

For a moment no words came out of my mouth. Then I took a deep breath and said in a rush, "Mom, where's the penny?"

"Penny?" Mom cried out. "What penny? Audrey, you're scaring me. What are you talking about?"

"The penny I gave you today, remember? Two dollars and one penny—for the Skittles bag!" My voice had taken on a desperate tone.

Mom put her fingers to her cheek. "I probably used it at the store today. Why?" She looked at me, genuinely worried.

I ignored her question. "Who did you give it to? Who?"

"I don't know—the person at the register!"

I let out my breath in a rush. She didn't have it. But what she said made me realize that someone else did. Someone else would be tormented by their nightmares. "What did he look like?" I persisted. I still had to find the penny.

"He was young. Brown hair, blue eyes. Tall. That's all I remember. Now Audrey, please tell me what's wrong!"

But I had already rushed away into my bedroom to ponder the situation and come up with a plan.

Chapter Seven

It wasn't until several hours later that I finally glanced out my window and noticed that the sun had long since set. Although it was already well into the evening, my heart had not quite stopped its frantic pounding from my recent scare.

Mom was fine. This realization extracted a long sigh of relief from me. It occurred to me then that Carson Gray hadn't known what he was talking about. It was just a rant about a penny that I just happened to find. I stood, stretching my legs a bit. This meant that nothing Carson had said was true. He had just been teasing me, taking me for a fool. It surprised me how easily he had convinced me that my mother was in danger, that a single penny lying on the wrong side could unlock terrible nightmares. It seemed ridiculous to me now, just thinking about it. I wasn't even a superstitious person, though most of the other citizens of Fortune couldn't say the same.

I was hurt. He had seemed like such a nice person. But I was relieved too.

One thought nudged at me persistently. If those nightmares from the penny were not real, then what about what *had* happened to me? What about my mishaps with the knife and the cliff? They had seemed to fit so well that they couldn't have been a coincidence...

I pulled my door open and stepped out into the hallway. I hadn't eaten for the better part of the day, and now I realized how hungry I was.

But in the hallway I stopped suddenly. Something wasn't right. It took me a minute to figure it out. It was too quiet. Usually I could hear Mom clattering around in the kitchen and Shelby meowing insistently for food, even though she would have just eaten. But there was nothing. Just silence.

"Mom?" I called out unsurely. My voice echoed through the hall. I turned the corner quickly and reached the living room.

"Audrey, get back!" Mom shouted at me, panic in her voice. The front door stood ajar, and Mom was plastered against the wall. For the first time I saw true, raw terror in her eyes. Her fear made me even more afraid. I followed her gaze, focusing on the floor. What I saw made my heart stop, and I backed away a step. There was a snake inside our house.

It was large for a snake and had patterns of light and dark brown on its skin. I stood motionless, gaping at the snake in the middle of the room.

"It's a rattlesnake, Audrey. It's poisonous!" Mom gasped, and I knew she was right. The rattlesnake flicked its tongue, shaking the rattle on its tail threateningly. Its beady eyes focused on my mother, not paying any attention to me.

Before I could do anything, the snake recoiled suddenly and lunged at Mom. She stumbled backwards into a side table, and the snake sank its fangs deep into her ankle.

I screamed and Mom made a small sound, gripping the arm of a chair and trying to back up. I lurched forward and brought my foot down on the snake's body, trying to squash it.

That was a mistake. The snake hissed sharply and turned its attention to me. I drew back quickly, and suddenly Mom was there. She had somehow gotten a large knife from the kitchen and now she flung it, aiming at the rattlesnake. The knife met its mark. The body of the rattlesnake lay writhing on the floor in front of us, completely severed from its head. I breathed a sigh of relief, but that relief was not long-lived. I gaped at the head of the snake as its eyes stared piercingly back at me. It flicked its forked tongue out at me, and I flinched and staggered back to Mom. She was pale and the fear had not left her eyes. "Mom, are you all right?" I asked her anxiously. "Let me see the bite!"

"I'm fine," she whispered, but when she peeled back her sock on her right foot, I gasped. Two small parallel lines ran deep on her ankle, and the skin around the bite had begun to turn a bruised red-and-purple color.

"I'm going to call 9-1-1," I announced, worried, and Mom didn't make any objections. I picked up the phone, and with a shaky voice, quickly explained to the dispatcher what had happened.

It took what felt like an eternity for the ambulance to arrive. While we waited, I washed the bite on Mom's ankle, but there wasn't much more I could do. They didn't let me go with her to the hospital, but that was okay with me. The hospital held too many bad memories.

After they took Mom away in the ambulance, Mrs. Tweedy came to the door. "Audrey, dearie, are you all right?" she asked in her high-pitched voice. "Poor girl! What happened to your mother — so dreadful!" Mrs. Tweedy rambled on for a few more minutes until she decided that I should stay at her house for the night. I didn't protest.

Half an hour later, I stood with Mrs. Tweedy in front of her house at the edge of town, not far from mine. "Now, come on in, sweetie," Mrs. Tweedy told me, climbing the stone steps to her house carefully. There were several other houses on either side of her pale pink home. As she opened the painted front door at the top of the steps, I noticed the rusty horseshoe hanging on it with the open side facing up for good luck, of course. I hadn't realized until now how superstitious our neighbors really were.

Mrs. Tweedy had begun to ramble on again, but I was only half listening. I was too worried about Mom. Would she be all right? I wanted to ask Mrs. Tweedy, but she wouldn't know any more than I did. It was completely dark outside, and had been for quite some time. It wasn't too much later that I climbed under the blankets Mrs. Tweedy had laid out on her couch for me, and I fell asleep, exhausted.

The next day Mom was released from the hospital. The hospital staff said that it was a "dry bite," that the venomous snake had "bitten her without envenoming." They said she was very lucky and that it was quite unusual for a rattlesnake to bite without injecting any venom. The doctors and nurses were perplexed, but I was just glad Mom was fine.

Chapter Eight

Jonathan waded through a pile of open books on his bedroom floor. It had gotten so bad that it was hard to get in through the door. He shook his head in dismay. His bedroom wasn't that big to begin with. Bedrooms in apartments never were, and the bathrooms were miniscule.

Jonathan lived in a third-floor apartment with his parents. They had only been in Fortune for a matter of months, and already Jonathan liked it. The only problem was that Fortune had only one library and one bookstore. And both were small, much to his disappointment.

He didn't know why his parents chose Fortune, of all places, for their new hometown. Maybe it was simply that Fortune was a safe haven from the noise of bigger cities. Both his mother and father had lost their jobs a year apart when they lived in Chicago. Now they both had full-time jobs (or several part-time ones, in his mother's case) here. Jonathan never saw much of either of them anymore. His mother was a daycare worker at Rainbow Children's Daycare and his father sorted mail at the post office. It wasn't much, they told him, but it was enough. They seemed perfectly happy with that.

Jonathan surveyed the books in his room. He owned most of them. They were about all sorts of things: from myths and legends to architecture and adventure stories — he was interested in them all. He was so interested, in fact, that he could never bring himself to put any of them away on the bookshelves where they belonged. Whenever he found a picture or paragraph that was particularly interesting (which happened to be quite often), he left it open on that page on whatever surface was available. Not only the floor, but also his desk and chair, and even his pillow were all currently being used as book space. It frustrated his mother and, sometimes, even him. Once, it took a whole forty-five minutes to find his book on global warming.

As Jonathan was clearing his bed of the pile of encyclopedias, and in the process, finding a long-lost origami snowman, the alarm on his wristwatch began to beep. Jonathan heaved a heavy sigh. The alarm signaled it was time to leave for his shift at the grocery store. He worked as a cashier there, and his boss certainly wouldn't appreciate it if he was late. With great reluctance, he pulled away from the piles of books in front of him and left the apartment.

✷✷✷

Jonathan stood outside the grocery store during his break, counting his money to see if he had enough for some bread and milk. These days he usually prepared his own meals, even dinner. His father worked late at the post office, and his mother had a part-time job in the evenings after parents picked up their kids from the daycare. He couldn't say he was an outstanding cook, but he knew how to make macaroni and cheese or spaghetti. In fact, he would probably have one of those for dinner tonight, he thought dejectedly.

He happened to look up at the place where the land dropped off into a steep cliff. A small red-haired girl was standing dangerously close to the edge. Jonathan recognized her as Audrey, one of the few names he remembered since moving to Fortune. He had seen her at the grocery store on several occasions during the first few weeks after his family had moved here. She had lingered around the ice cream freezer doors.

Jonathan eyed her, wondering why she was standing so close. She must be pretty brave to do that, he thought.

When he saw her lose her footing he jumped into action. He reached her and skidded to a stop, also dangerously close to falling. He grabbed her arm and quickly pulled her up. He was breathing hard from the effort, but fortunately she wasn't very heavy.

When they were both farther away from the overhang, Jonathan allowed himself to think.

Audrey had two different colored eyes. He thought that was quite unique. She was so lucky she stood out from everyone else — unlike him. Even just standing next to her made him feel so *normal*.

They talked for a few awkward moments, then Jonathan excused himself. After he left Audrey, Jonathan looked at his watch. Unfortunately, his break had ended. He usually bought food for dinner during his last break, but now he would have to take care of that when his shift was over. He resumed his place at Register 2 and began his routine of scanning items for each person in line. Jonathan distractedly rang up the amount for the first person in line, gave her the change from the cash register and told her to have a nice day. When he looked up a few seconds later, she was still there. It was Ms. Feller from the bakery. She tightened her high ponytail and informed him, "You gave me $16 in change. You only owed me $4.60."

Jonathan checked and discovered his mistake. He was surprised she had the honesty to tell him. It seemed he just couldn't keep his mind on his work. It wasn't every day you saved someone from a fifty-foot fall, after all.

After ringing up several customers, making sure to double-check each transaction, he recognized an all too familiar face. The man stood tall and solemn, clothed in all black. "Hi there, Uncle Viktor. Did you find everything okay?" Jonathan asked his routine question. Viktor Sharpe's face darkened until it was almost a deep shade of purple, resembling an overripe plum. "*Never* call me that," he said to Jonathan. "Sharpe. Call me Sharpe."

"If you say so, *Uncle* Sharpe." Sharpe was Jonathan's father's half-brother. Not that anyone could ever tell. The two were totally different. Jonathan's father worked a lot, but also joked and laughed often, like Jonathan. Uncle Sharpe, though, kept to himself and rarely even smiled. When he did, it was more like a smirk, as if he knew something you didn't. It was a creepy feeling.

Before this encounter, Jonathan hadn't seen

him for about two years. His father said Sharpe traveled a lot, and it wasn't unusual for years to go by without seeing Sharpe or anyone knowing even in general where he was.

Sharpe was the strange one in the family, there was no doubt about that. It wouldn't surprise Jonathan if not even Sharpe's own father knew him well. So why was he here in the only town for miles?

"I didn't come here to buy food," Sharpe told him dryly. Jonathan realized it was true; he didn't have a grocery cart.

"Then what are you here for?" Jonathan asked him squarely.

Sharpe narrowed his eyes and Jonathan had the strangest feeling that Sharpe didn't particularly like him. "I came to speak with you."

"Me?"

"Yes, you. Who else?" He looked down at Jonathan as if he was a little kid who needed everything carefully explained to him. Then Sharpe's eyes darted around furtively, and he uncharacteristically hesitated. "Perhaps we could speak somewhere a bit more...private?"

"Um, sure." Jonathan didn't bother to hide his surprise, or annoyance. He led his uncle to the storage room in the back, hoping to get this done quickly. He could lose his job if his boss realized he had abandoned his register.

Jonathan pulled out two dusty crates to sit on. Sharpe wrinkled his nose in distaste at the less-than-magnificent seating, and Jonathan thought for a minute he would refuse and just stand against the wall stoically. When he finally did sit down, Jonathan sat as well.

Sharpe was the first to speak. "You are likely wondering why I am here. I see that you have a job at this supermarket. It doesn't pay much."

Jonathan nodded in silent confirmation and pulled his lips together tightly. Where was he going with this?

"I am in need of an assistant, perhaps an apprentice. Yes, I suppose one could call it that," Sharpe mused. "You are a relatively intelligent child. You would earn quite a bit more than a mere check-out boy, of course."

Jonathan's eyebrows drew together as he thought. From the corner of his eye he could see his uncle, tapping his fingers in impatience. "Well, what exactly is it you do?" he questioned his uncle. He hadn't even known Sharpe had a job.

Sharpe pursed his lips in annoyance at the question. "I work and do research in the mystical arts. I will train you in that subject. Your tasks will not be hard, I assure you, if that is what you are concerned with."

Jonathan wondered what the mystical arts were. Were they like magic? Somehow, he couldn't imagine his serious uncle pulling a rabbit out of a hat.

"I have spoken with your parents and they have already agreed," Sharpe informed him.

That came as a surprise. "All right," he consented. He could use the extra money, and if his parents were fine with it then why not?

"Good." A corner of Sharpe's mouth turned up slightly. "We shall begin immediately."

"Okay. Wait. What? What about my job here? I need to get back to my register!"

"Very well," Sharpe frowned darkly. "I will arrange the situation with your boss."

Before he could say anything, Sharpe swept out of the room. Jonathan stood up, brows knitted in utter confusion. What had he gotten himself into?

Within moments Sharpe returned wearing a look of satisfaction. "I spoke with your boss. As of now, you no longer work at this disgusting place." He wrinkled his nose in emphasis.

"What?" Something was unsettling about all of this. How had his uncle done that so quickly? What *had* he gotten himself into?

✳✳✳

Fifteen minutes later, Jonathan found himself in a very small darkened building in the less populated part of town. Jonathan supposed it must be Sharpe's house, although he hadn't thought of his uncle as owning a home. He traveled so much he didn't really need a place to come back to.

Sharpe led Jonathan through a doorway. They were now in a narrow hallway, so narrow that only one person could pass at a time. Sharpe switched on the lights but they flickered and dimmed, providing only a bare minimum of illumination. In fact, the shadows were so thick Jonathan couldn't tell what colors the hall walls were painted. He could see there weren't any pictures or decorations on them, though. They were completely blank.

Sharpe turned left into a different hallway and shoved open two double doors. Jonathan squinted at the sudden explosion of light. Once his eyes adjusted they widened in astonishment.

The room was huge and Jonathan wondered how it could possibly fit in such a miniscule house. The ceiling rose at least twenty feet above their heads and hanging from it were dozens of luminous overhead lights, each brightening a specific area. Wall sconces and shiny wood paneling gave the room an old-fashioned feel, but they contrasted strangely with all of the technology that dominated the room. He recognized a row of high-tech-looking computers that lined one wall, but almost everything else he saw was beyond his comprehension. To Jonathan, the room resembled a mad scientist's laboratory (without the beakers and strange concoctions).

Flat screens were built into many countertops next to the computers, and a steady whirring filled the room. What baffled Jonathan was the machinery in the center of the room. The metal machines were sleek and shiny, with wires and buttons protruding from nearly every surface. Jonathan had never seen anything like them before. But what exactly *were* they? He stepped forward, eager to take a closer look—to study each piece separately.

"Don't touch anything!" Sharpe ordered, suddenly more menacing than he had been before. Startled, Jonathan stepped back, and Sharpe's anger deflated.

"What is all this?" Jonathan asked. He wanted to be cautious but he allowed his curiosity to take over.

"This is my equipment. It's what has brought me this far in my research."

Jonathan looked around once more and took it all in. He had so many questions, but suspected his uncle would merely deflect them with a wave of his hand. But if Sharpe wasn't going to tell him anything, why did he bother making Jonathan his assistant?

Jonathan opened his mouth to speak, perhaps to voice some bold question, but Sharpe began first. "I suppose we should start with something relatively simple. There is much you need to learn, boy — an enormous amount to learn if you are going to be the least bit useful to me."

Jonathan wove his fingers through his hair, indignant at the last remark, but said nothing. Sometimes it paid to be silent, especially with such an irascible man.

"Well then," Sharpe proceeded, "let me see… Now tell me, just how superstitious are you?"

Jonathan was caught off guard by the unexpected question. "Uh, not much, I think. I mean, I don't usually avoid black cats or stepping on cracks if that's what you mean."

"Interesting. That's reasonable, I suppose. You don't strike me as that type of person."

Jonathan wondered what kind of person his uncle did think he was, but he had no intention of asking.

"What if I were to tell you that superstitious people have quite valid reasons for believing as they do?"

Jonathan was shocked. "Are you telling me all those sayings are true? If I step on a crack I'll break my mother's back?" he challenged, referring to the popular children's rhyme.

Sharpe scoffed, "Most likely not, no. But take, for example, the popular myth about the Empire State Building. No doubt you've heard about it. It states that if one drops a penny off of the Empire State Building it can kill a person or perhaps total a car. This, of course, sounds like blasphemy to some. Most scientists agree that even with the force and distance of the fall from that height, there would be no danger of injury. Because a penny is lightweight and not aerodynamic, air resistance slows it down so much that its terminal velocity is quite low.

"However, I did conduct an experiment myself. You see, if darkness enters an object such as a penny, it grows more powerful. It can even kill. I was able to test that theory from the top of that building."

Jonathan had been listening with widened eyes, though his confusion was evident. Then he had a startling thought: *What if my uncle is a murderer; his weapon, a penny?*

"Unfortunately," Sharpe continued, oblivious to Jonathan's thoughts, "I was only able to hit a street sign and, alas, it ended up too damaged to be salvaged," he sighed woefully. "But even so, it was a highly informative excursion," Sharpe concluded.

"I don't understand," Jonathan broke in when Sharpe seemed to be finished with his monologue. "You said you put darkness in a penny. But what does that mean? How is that even physically possible?"

Sharpe put a hand to his head as if Jonathan's questions were giving him a headache. Jonathan didn't care. He wanted to know. He *had* to know.

Seeing his determination, Sharpe reluctantly spoke again. "I think it best that you do not fully understand that. However, I shall tell you this. A little bit of darkness lies in everything—people and objects alike. With knowledge and ability, a person can control it and mold it to his will. But if one wished to obtain a much larger quantity of darkness one would have to find Pandora's box, the original source of darkness on Earth in the first place."

Sharpe suddenly stopped and gave Jonathan a piercing look. "Now, you must not speak to anyone of what you have seen or heard in this room, not even to your parents," he ordered. "Swear to it!"

"Okay, I swear!" promised Jonathan quickly.

"Good. I shall know if you do." Jonathan held out his hand and Sharpe grudgingly shook it, pulling away quickly.

"You shall not be paid for today," Sharpe announced, much to Jonathan's dismay. "You did not do anything. However, return on Wednesday and we will put your new knowledge to good use."

****

Back in his apartment less than an hour later, Jonathan pondered all that his uncle had told him. Could it possibly be that he was telling the truth? Or had Sharpe turned into a raving lunatic since anyone had last seen him? And what did Sharpe want Jonathan for?

In his bedroom, Jonathan ducked his head down and peered under his bed and bedside table. Where was that book? Finally he found what he was looking for. From under a pile of short story collections he produced a heavy book with a golden cover. *Tales of Greek Mythology.*

He flipped to the table of contents and found the section about Pandora's box. It was one of the first myths in the book. Jonathan began to read.

> *The myth of Pandora's box, or Pandora's jar, as it is more accurately titled, is one of the*

most popular and well-known stories of Greek mythology. It tells of the first mortal woman, the beautiful young lady named Pandora, and the great mistake her curiosity led her to make.

When a man named Prometheus stole fire from Mount Olympus to give to the mortals, the powerful god Zeus became angry and ordered the rest of the gods to create a woman as punishment to all mankind. Each god or goddess bestowed upon the woman a gift, like great beauty and a powerful curiosity. They named the woman Pandora, meaning "all gifted."

Zeus gave Pandora to Epimetheus, Prometheus's brother, as a gift. Prometheus had warned his brother not to accept any gifts from Zeus because they could be a trick, but Epimetheus did not listen. He accepted and Pandora became his wife.

Zeus then gave Epimetheus and Pandora a box (in some accounts, a jar) and told them they mustn't ever open it. Each day Pandora walked by the box and wondered what could be inside. She thought it foolish never to be able to see the gift Zeus had given them.

One day Pandora's curiosity got the best of her and she opened the box, just as Zeus had known she would. As soon as she took off the lid, monsters flew out at her. They were Disease, Envy, War, Hate, Nightmares, and Misfortune. Pandora gasped and slammed the lid shut, but it was too late. All of the evils no one had ever before seen had escaped into the world.

Then Pandora heard a little sound from inside the box. She opened it cautiously and peeked inside. Still trapped in the box was a single bug. It was Hope. Pandora set Hope free, because only would all of these troubles be bearable if there, too, was Hope.

Jonathan closed the book with a snap. His uncle had said that Pandora's box held a lot of darkness, but if the myth was true, then wasn't the box now empty? Maybe someone had caught some of the evil released from the box and locked it back in. Sharpe honestly seemed to think Pandora's box truly existed. Was he looking for it? And if so, why?

Chapter Nine

I was splayed out on my beanbag chair, staring into empty space. I had been like this for the past several hours, and I was ready for a break from thinking.

Several days had come and gone since the rattlesnake had bitten Mom, but I hadn't gone to see Carson yet. I had thought before that there wasn't any need to—that he was nothing but a charlatan. But now I didn't think so. The incident with the snake had convinced me that Carson spoke the truth. The penny I had picked up really was bringing nightmares to life. There was no other way to explain it. I buried my face in my hands. I had messed up—it was entirely my fault. I should never have given Mom that penny. If I hadn't, none of this would have happened. I needed to do something to fix this, but I had no idea what.

My eyes shifted and landed on the Fortune snow globe. A sudden memory flew up and hit me hard.

***

We were in the hospital. The smell of antiseptic and the white of the walls made my head throb, and the rushing and loud voices disoriented me. Bits of hurried conversations echoed in my head: "…in critical condition…sudden heart attack…chances are slim…"

Nurses wheeled Dad past us and into a different room, and I cried out. Mom held me back and tried to speak to me in low, soothing tones, but she couldn't keep the tears from her eyes.

"Dad!" I screamed, trying to fight Mom's arms around me. The door shut decisively, and I could no longer see him.

The waiting was the worst. It felt like hours, sitting there in the waiting room with Mom. "I want to see him!" I sobbed over and over again.

At one point, Mom left me with my aunt. I sat there in the waiting room, waiting for her to come back. When she finally did, her face was tearstained. "He's gone," she whispered brokenly.

***

I gasped and blinked rapidly, trying to shake the memory away. Without realizing it, I had gotten up and was pacing the length of my room. I stopped, letting out a long, shaky breath. I needed to get outside.

As I opened my bedroom door, the only sounds I heard were the ticking of the kitchen clock and an airplane rumbling somewhere far above in the clouds. Mom must have left for work already. She insisted that she was well enough to go to work and I had to admit, she did seem fine. The two thin lines on her ankle were the only sign of what had happened. The snake bite wasn't infected at all, so Mom saw no reason to stay home and rest. I was glad I was on fall break from school. With everything going on, I wouldn't be able to concentrate on my schoolwork.

I grabbed a neon-green sticky note from a drawer and wrote a quick note in case Mom got back early. Sticking it on the kitchen table at her spot, I slipped out the back door, not bothering to lock it. Unconsciously, I started up the path toward town. Ahh. The crisp air felt so good against my skin. I breathed in deeply and savored the feel of the slight breeze on my face.

"Audrey!" A cheerful voice called out, breaking me from my reverie.

I looked up, filled with surprise. "Carson, what are you doing here?"

He walked down the path toward me. I wasn't used to seeing him anywhere other than the water fountain. It was as though he lived there.

"I wanted to see if you were all right. When I didn't hear anything from you after you went home to find your mother, I became a bit worried."

Guilt ebbed its way inside me. I should have gone to see him earlier.

"Do you know of someplace quiet where we can talk?" Carson asked me. "The fountain in the shopping square isn't exactly the most private place." He smiled at me as if he could tell I needed it.

"Sure, I think I know a place," I said, and turned in the opposite direction. As we walked, I tried to explain what I had found out from Mom. "When I got home, I asked Mom about the penny and she didn't have it. She said she used it to pay at the

store. I'm so sorry I didn't tell you before, I just—"
I broke off, not knowing how to finish the sentence.
"Then Mom was attacked by a rattlesnake. It's the
one thing I know she's really afraid of. She's fine
now, but with that and the knife and the cliff..."

Carson patted my back and looked at me with
sympathy. "I heard about what happened to your
mother. That was a lot for you to go through—you
and your mother. I'm glad to hear she seems to be
just fine. But I agree with you. What happened is
no coincidence. It is the doing of the dark presence
in the penny."

Now I was confused. "But the snake didn't
attack Mom until after she had already given the
penny to someone else. That doesn't make sense."

Carson thought for a while. "Sometimes a little
bit of the essence contained in the penny lingers
after the coin has been passed on. Perhaps that is
what happened, but..."

"What?"

He looked at me. "The experiences from your
nightmare tell me that it wasn't just a little bit
leftover from the penny. Whatever that penny
holds is very powerful."

We were both silent for a few moments. Then
Carson spoke again. "Did she say who the cashier
was?"

It took me a moment to realize he was talking
about the cashier Mom had given the penny to.
"Only that he was young with brown hair and blue
eyes. I don't know who that could be."

"Hmm," Carson murmured.

"It would be practically impossible to find the
penny again. I don't know that there's anything we
can do about it, right?"

"Maybe there is, maybe there isn't," Carson speculated.

We arrived at the clearing and stepped inside. I had never shown this spot to anyone else before, so I self-consciously hung back to let him take it all in. More leaves had fallen, and it was even more beautiful than when I had last seen it.

"This truly is a wondrous place of yours, Audrey," Carson told me. "Keep it close to your heart."

I didn't know what to say to that, so I stayed silent. We found seats on fallen logs. There were more fallen trees than I remembered.

"So what was it you wanted to talk to me about?" I asked Carson after we had settled down.

"What?" He turned toward me, confused.

"Didn't you want to talk about something without anyone else around?" Now I was confused.

"Oh, yes." He drew the words out as if he wasn't quite sure what to say next. "I'm sorry I didn't tell you this before Audrey, but the nightmares in the penny you found distracted me. I do feel obligated to tell you, since I began to the day we met."

I was startled. "Is this about why you said I was special?" I took a wild guess.

He nodded. "I noticed it as soon as I first saw you, but at first I thought you knew."

"Knew what?" I almost shrieked.

"I think there might be something you can do about the nightmares the penny has awoken. I don't know any better way to say it, Audrey, so I'll just tell you plainly. I believe you have an unusual ability that is really quite rare. If what I think is true, you're a dreamweaver."

I stared at him. Had I heard correctly? Was he

teasing me? I looked closely at Carson's worn face. He was serious. He totally believed what he said. I decided to believe it too.

"So, what exactly is a dreamweaver?"

He heaved a great breath and began. "A dreamweaver is a person who is able to create dreams using only her imagination. That is where the name comes from. In a way, a dreamweaver weaves dreams, but not for herself. She can create them for anyone. A dreamweaver can weave sweet dreams or nightmares. The choice is hers. It is a great—and dangerous—power to hold."

I blinked. After hearing that, I wouldn't have been surprised if he told me that I could fly, too. Then I realized something. "Wait, if dreamweavers are so uncommon, how can they weave so many dreams? I mean, everyone has dreams. Some people dream every single night."

"Ah, yes, that is certainly a good point. The dreamweaver population has declined so much in the past few years that very few dreams are freshly woven. Instead, most people's dreams are now mere memories. You've probably had the same dream more than once before, right?"

I nodded, remembering a particular dream I'd had when I was little. It had something to do with monsters that slept on my bed and made me sleep underneath it. I'd had that dream for several months in a row. I always ended up tangled in a blanket on the floor when I awoke in the morning.

"Well, that often happens with dreams. The others are just memories of the original dream along with a few things your brain adds. Also, recently I've heard that more and more dreams are simply memories of another dream woven for someone else."

"So people have the same dreams as other people?"

"Yes, but they're always just a tiny bit different. Each person dreams them a little differently."

This was a lot to take in for one day. "But how do you know all of this? Are you a dreamweaver too?"

Carson hesitated for a second, then chuckled. "Oh, no. I'm what you would call a dream sender. I channel a dream into a person's mind once a dreamweaver weaves it. We need a dreamweaver to do our job. But, to give you a little perspective, I'd say there is, oh, maybe one dreamweaver for every seventy-five dream senders now."

I was shocked. "I guess you don't get to do your job much, huh?"

"No," Carson smiled. "I haven't met a dreamweaver in twenty years." For a moment he seemed lost in the past, his eyes glazed with a faraway look. Then he suddenly refocused on me. "I will teach you how to dreamweave, if you like. I should warn you though, it is difficult."

"Can I do it now?" I jumped up, excited.

"I suppose if you're that eager to..." Carson teased.

"What do I do first?"

"Well, I think the first time we should just see if you can summon your power. Sit back down; it's easier that way."

I did, and my nerves finally caught up with my excitement. I knew it was silly, but what if I somehow messed up?

"Now, the idea is simple, but it takes a lot of

mental focus," Carson was saying. "Your mind will be doing most of the work. All right, let's go ahead and try. First you need to block out everything around you and concentrate very hard on what you want to do."

I took a deep breath and closed my eyes. What *did* I want to do, exactly?

"Think only of the power you want to let loose. Pull it out from deep inside you. Don't get distracted. Let those thoughts fill your mind."

I was scrunching up my nose in concentration! How could I be distracted? I opened one eye slightly and looked at Carson through the slit. He was watching me closely. "Concentrate," he reminded me.

I obeyed and sat there waiting. Without a warning, warmth pulsed through my veins and a tingling sensation ran up and down my arms. I gasped. The feeling faded and I opened my eyes fully. "Nothing?" I asked Carson, disappointed.

He shook his head. "For a moment I thought you got something, though."

"I thought so too," I remarked, thinking of the strange feeling that went through me.

"Don't worry," Carson reassured me, "It's quite difficult to dreamweave for the first time."

"Carson," I asked him, "what if you were wrong about me?"

He set his mouth into a firm line of determination. "I'm not."

Chapter Ten

Narrow, beady eyes stared at Jonathan, who was standing on Sharpe's porch step. "Hello, Uncle Sharpe," Jonathan said coolly. He moved to slip into the house, eager to see Sharpe's equipment again, but Sharpe stopped him.

"There will be no need to enter today," he said coldly. "I have an outdoor assignment for you. Let us take...a little walk."

Jonathan reluctantly agreed, wondering what his uncle had in mind. Something about this made him a little uneasy.

As soon as they began to walk, Jonathan keeping pace with Sharpe's long strides, Sharpe began to speak. "Surely you remember what I have told you about darkness."

Jonathan nodded, but Sharpe was not looking at him.

"I have not told you how I know about darkness in the first place."

Jonathan perked up. He had been wondering about that.

"I suppose now is the time to tell you what it is I do. Surely you recognized my navigation system in my house. I use it to track darkness. Despite what you may think, darkness is not bad, merely powerful. All my life I have searched for Pandora's box. I will teach you more about darkness, but first, as I've already mentioned, I have a task for you. Ah, yes, she should be right around here."

He and Sharpe turned a corner and Jonathan noticed Sharpe's upper lip curl. "It is ridiculous. I can sense her from a mile away."

For a moment Jonathan didn't know who his uncle was talking about. They were standing near some shops in town, including the bookstore, and Jonathan wished he could go inside for just a moment. Then he looked around and noticed a girl with flaming red hair.

The red-haired girl was talking to an older lady with a peacock feather hat. The girl turned slightly and Jonathan noticed with surprise that it was Audrey, the girl who had almost fallen off the cliff. He looked back and forth between her and Sharpe. It was clear that Sharpe was staring intently at Audrey. Then Jonathan started. Did he see a glint of fear in his uncle's eyes? No, when he looked again, Sharpe's face was expressionless. He must have been mistaken.

"Do you see that girl over there?" Sharpe asked, nodding in Audrey's general direction. Without waiting for an answer, he continued. "The girl is a danger to everyone around her. She is unusually powerful. She can destroy this whole town on a whim if she pleases. Normally, I'd ask you to stay away from her, but she has something I require. It is vital for my…research."

Audrey? Dangerous? Jonathan thought she seemed nice enough when he talked to her. Could she really be someone to be wary of? "How can you tell? That she's dangerous, I mean."

Sharpe turned on him. "Do you doubt me?" he accused. "Her eyes give her away. They are two different colors. That is the case for all those like her. In addition, if you look closely at her hair you will find that some of it is of a golden color. Her power has not fully developed yet, but she is still a great danger to those around her." Sharpe lifted his chin and studied Audrey from across the street. "What I want you to do for the next few weeks is get to know the girl. See if anything unusual slips from her mouth."

Jonathan was shocked. "What, so I'm just supposed to walk up to her and say, 'Hi, I'm stalking you. Would you like to be my friend?' "

"Anything to gain her trust," Sharpe growled, irritated. "We need her to trust you."

His uncle not-so-gently prodded Jonathan, causing him to jerk forward. Jonathan took a few more steps and miraculously ended up across the street. His brain was whirring at a hundred miles per hour and he couldn't think straight. He didn't fully believe Sharpe, but what if he was telling the truth?

Audrey had just finished talking to the other lady and turned, noticing him after a moment.

"Hi. I'm Jonathan. Remember me?" He grimaced. How was *that* for a reintroduction?

"Rescuer of poor girls who fall off cliffs," she laughed, and after a moment Jonathan joined in. "I remember."

Jonathan wasn't quite sure what to say next.

How exactly was he supposed to make her trust him? Audrey still seemed nothing more than friendly. Was she really that good of an actress?

"I never got to repay you for saving me," Audrey was saying. "What do you think about ice cream from Millie's? My treat."

Jonathan was thinking of a polite way to decline when he remembered he was actually *supposed* to be talking to Audrey, not looking at history books at the bookstore, which his mind kept returning to. Then he realized what she had said. "Ice cream? At this time of year?" He laughed, then gulped suddenly and stopped, hoping he hadn't insulted her. His uncle hadn't given him many details. She could be a murderer, for all he knew. But he was still doubtful.

To his relief, Audrey grinned. "It's never too cold for ice cream. In fact, I could really go for a chocolate fudge brownie cone about now."

Chapter Eleven

As we entered the ice cream shop a few stores down, a bell on the door rang. "Hi there, Audrey!" a voice called out, and I recognized the girl at the counter. Sara also had a part-time job at the clothing store next door.

I returned the greeting and stepped up to the counter, Jonathan following me.

"The usual for you?" Sara guessed, and I nodded.

As she deftly scooped balls of ice cream into a cone Sara commented, "I swear, you've been my only customer in the past month!" She handed me the cone and turned to Jonathan curiously. "I don't believe I know you."

"Oh." Jonathan looked up as if he had been startled from his thoughts. "I'm Jonathan. I just moved here not too long ago." He reached across the counter and shook her left hand, since her right was still holding the ice cream scooper. He glanced at the labels on the glass over each flavor. "I'll just have chocolate, please."

"Coming right up."

Jonathan and I sat at a table while Sara disappeared into a room in the back. We were the only ones left in the store. "So how do you like Fortune so far?" I asked, trying to start a conversation.

"It's great." Jonathan bit off a chunk of ice cream from the top of his cone. "I don't know that many people yet, though. It seems like Fortune is one of those towns where everybody knows everybody."

"That seems about right," I confirmed.

"So who was that lady you were standing with earlier out by the street?"

I was confused for a moment until he added, "With that peacock feather in her hat."

"Oh!" I laughed. "That's Mrs. Tweedy. She's a bit nosy, but sweet once you get to know her. She heard a rumor that I can speak Japanese and she asked me about it."

His eyebrows rose. "Can you?"

"Nope, and I don't plan to learn. I don't even *look* Japanese!"

"Konnichiwa."

"Excuse me?" I retorted.

"That means hello," he explained. "Or technically, more like good day."

I was surprised. "So *you* know Japanese?"

He looked sheepish. "I taught myself a little from a book. A couple of other languages, too."

There was a pause when neither of us said anything. My gaze turned to the window next to us, and it was then that something occurred to me. "This is going to sound a little crazy," I warned Jonathan, but he nodded for me to continue. "A while ago my mom was at the grocery store and she paid with some change." I paused, wondering how

I was going to say this without sounding completely psychotic. "One of the coins she used, a penny, is kind of…special. She described the cashier she gave it to. I was just wondering if maybe you were the cashier." I chewed at my lip, hoping he wouldn't laugh. It made me sound like I was attached to a mere penny, for goodness' sake!

He didn't laugh. Rather, he looked thoughtful. "I did work there as a cashier up until a few days ago when my uncle got me fired. But I don't know if I saw your mom. I wouldn't recognize her if I did."

I attempted to describe her, and Jonathan began to nod slowly. "I think I know who you mean. I remember because she only paid in coins, and it took forever to count out ten dollars' worth."

I smiled wryly. "Yes, that's my mom for you."

"So what's the deal with the penny though? Was it rare or something?" He watched me with interest.

"I guess you could say that. The thing is, I kind of need it back. What did you do with it?"

He shrugged. "It's hard to know where it is now. I probably gave it to a customer as change or someone else did after I left. I doubt it's still in the cash register. I'm sorry if it meant something to you," he added without a hint of sarcasm.

My heart sank, and I slumped down in my seat. How would I ever be able to find that unlucky penny now? Carson was right. It had gotten passed around, and now it was changing hands throughout the town. I didn't know what this would mean, but it couldn't be good. "Did you feel anything strange when my mom gave it to you?"

He furrowed his brow. "Not that I remember. Why? It's not cursed, is it?"

It took me a moment to realize he was only

kidding. I tried to join in his laughter, but all I could manage was a shaky giggle that sounded more like a sob. He had no idea how close to the truth he was.

I threw the rest of my cone in the trash, watching it plummet down the short distance in slow motion. It reminded me of my dreams—my nightmares. I was falling, always falling. The whole town was falling into a dark abyss. The problem was I had no idea where we would land when we finally reached the bottom.

Chapter Twelve

"Good. Very good," Carson praised. We were sitting in the clearing, and I was trying to dreamweave again. Or at least summon the power inside me that I needed for it. I was finally able to do it, if only for a short time. Power radiated inside me and it felt as if it was warm, golden sunshine.

If there had ever been any doubt that I was a dreamweaver it was gone now. Once I did it the first time, it wasn't difficult to do it again. I couldn't explain it, but I was somehow able to reach deep inside myself and come out with energy dripping from my fingertips. I felt, well, powerful.

I let it fade away and Carson clapped heartily. "See, I knew you could do it!" He held up his hand for a high-five and I slapped it lightly, grinning from ear to ear. I couldn't help it; it felt so amazing.

"I think it's time you tried something harder," Carson told me. "You're ready to start dreamweaving."

Before I could jump up and down clapping,

or protest that I needed more time (I hadn't decided which yet), something white and furry dropped from a tree branch above and landed on my head. "Eek!" I screamed while Carson tried unsuccessfully not to laugh.

"I suppose that must be your cat," he observed.

"Shelby!" I shrieked as she stepped onto my shoulder and gracefully jumped into a pile of leaves on the ground. She licked her paw innocently and strolled over to a spot with a patch of light on the ground. She curled up and immediately fell fast asleep.

I shook my head, smiling. "Yes, that's my cat," I told Carson. "I don't know how she found me here. She must've slipped out the back door when I left and I didn't notice."

"That's perfectly fine," Carson assured me. "She can help us. You can try to dreamweave for her while she's asleep."

"Not a nightmare!" I said quickly, but I needn't have worried.

"Of course not. I wouldn't want you to weave a nightmare anyway. Unfortunately, some dreamweavers choose to. I've met dreamweavers in the past that...didn't make the best decisions. I've told you that a dreamweaver can weave both good dreams and nightmares. It is up to you to choose which path you'll take. Are you ready to try?"

I nodded. I couldn't mess up and somehow hurt Shelby could I? She was annoying, but not *that* annoying.

"Okay, summon the energy from within you," Carson instructed. "We'll take it one step at a time. If you don't feel comfortable at any time, you can just back out." Instead of reassuring me, what he said frightened me. I reached inside myself and pulled. My fingertips tingled and I looked over at Carson.

"All right, very good. Now, I'm a dream sender, not a dreamweaver, so I'm not sure exactly how this works. Think of something you want Shelby to dream about. Remember, it should be happy."

I pictured a field of long grass like the one behind our house. It played in my mind like a movie. A mouse darted around thick blades of grass, and Shelby followed close behind. I thought that was an appropriate dream for a cat.

The tingling sent shivers down my body, and a shrill ringing filled my ears. I could barely hear Carson speaking, even though he had probably raised his voice a bit.

"You need to intertwine a strand of the energy inside you with the dream you want to make. It needs to be woven. Just think about what you want it to do!"

Somehow, I felt a tiny strand unraveling from the ball of energy inside me. I had no idea what I was supposed to do, and tried to tell Carson so. No words came out of my mouth. I thought intently about the dream and golden strand interlocking and weaving. To my utter surprise, I could suddenly feel it happening inside me. It felt like something moving underneath my skin—a combination of liquid and vapor. "I think I have it!" I shouted to Carson.

"Good! Transfer it to me now so I can channel it to your cat."

I reached out blindly and felt the large, wrinkled hand grab mine. The dream flowed through me and into Carson's outstretched arm with a burst and crackle of energy. I couldn't tell what Carson did then, but blurred light swirled through the air around him and suddenly vanished.

I released his hand and stumbled backward. I found a large rock and sat down on it, breathing hard. I felt drained and exhausted. Carson was still standing and smiling proudly.

"Did we do it? Did it work?" I asked eagerly.

"We sure did!" Carson exclaimed. "Look at your cat."

I turned and looked at Shelby. Her eyes were still shut, but every now and then she shifted positions. Her front paw was outstretched, and it looked as though she was unconsciously batting at something on the ground.

Crunch! Both Carson and I looked up at the unexpected noise. It wasn't Shelby; she was still curled up in one of the few spots on the ground that was bare of leaves.

"Who's there?" Carson called out sharply.

For a moment no one appeared, but then a figure stepped out from behind the trunk of a tree. My eyes widened. "Jonathan?"

Jonathan came closer and then backed up a step. "I—I'm sorry," he stammered, "I heard voices..." he trailed off and looked over at me. A mixture of expressions flitted across his face. Confusion. Guilt. And, fear?

In a gentle voice Carson scolded, "I suppose you've been listening a while, son." Jonathan nodded sheepishly.

"Did you see—" I began, and Jonathan nodded again.

"I'm really sorry," he repeated. "I didn't mean to. I mean, I'm not going to tell anybody."

Carson started to interject but I stopped him. "It's okay Carson, this is Jonathan. I trust him."

Carson thought for a moment, and then seemed to accept what I said. "This is serious though," he addressed Jonathan, "Don't try to get anyone else involved. It seems like now *you* are involved."

Jonathan turned to me. "So you can really make dreams?"

The realization of how much he had seen struck me hard. I wasn't worried about him telling anyone else; no one would believe him anyway. But I had thought of him as a kind of friend, and I didn't have many. What would he think of me now?

He instantly answered my unspoken question without meaning to. "That is so cool!" he exclaimed. "How does it work? Is the cerebrum involved in the process?"

I looked at Carson. "Honestly, I have no idea." I was surprised at his enthusiasm. Carson shook his head, indicating that he did not know either.

Jonathan stayed for the next hour. He asked me to show him dreamweaving (up close this time), and I did, feeling only slightly uncomfortable. I was able to do it again, which made me confident that I had a little more control over my ability.

Carson was kind while Jonathan was there, if a bit wary. I didn't blame him, but I was glad there was one more person who knew about what I could do. I didn't like not being able to tell my mom. I hated keeping secrets from her, but she was so practical and sensible I didn't think she would believe me if I told her.

As we were finishing for the day, Jonathan spoke up again. "So does all of this have something to do with that penny you were asking me about?"

I exchanged a glance with Carson, who raised his eyebrows in surprise. How was it that Jonathan was smart enough to connect my dreamweaving with something I had barely mentioned once? Even I could hardly keep all the facts straight in my mind.

"Yes, it is true that we are looking for a penny," Carson answered for me. "It contains an evil that targets its possessors. Audrey and I are attempting to find it and destroy it before it can do much harm."

I wasn't sure how much Jonathan believed of what Carson said, but Jonathan said earnestly, "Well, I just want to tell you that I'll help with anything you need."

***

Jonathan soon left, and Carson turned to me. "Well, I think we accomplished quite a bit for one day, don't you think?" he asked.

I agreed. "Carson," I began, "where did the nightmares from the penny come from?"

Carson sighed. "Have you ever heard of Pandora's box?" he asked me.

I nodded. I had learned about it last year at school. The Greeks believed it was the source of all evil.

"Well, it's not just a story," Carson told me. "It really does exist. Long ago, a powerful dreamweaver was able to banish some of the evil that escaped and return it to the box. The evil was Nightmares. Since then, the only nightmares that plague the world are the ones that other dreamweavers created afterward from next to nothing." He let out a long breath. "I think some of the nightmares that were returned to the box were released into the penny when it landed on tails."

✳✳✳

Much later, I was still in the clearing thinking about what Carson had said before he left. I was alone now, and I turned in a slow circle, inhaling the crispness of fall. I tried to imagine Pandora's box, dirty and rotted with age, buried somewhere deep within the earth. It was hard to think of something so evil resting under a surface that held so much of nature's beauty.

I glanced around looking for Shelby but didn't see her. She must have returned home. She wasn't really an outdoor cat, but she knew her way around the area as well as I did.

I plodded through the grass back toward home. Each step meant I had to lift my feet about a foot off the ground to wade through the swaying grass, but I didn't mind.

The back of the cottage came in sight, and I picked up my pace. I jumped over the picket fence easily since it was so small. We didn't have a gate for the backyard.

The back door was unlocked like always, and I stepped onto the hard tile of the kitchen floor. As the door swung shut with a click, I kicked off my shoes and walked across the ice cold tiles in my bare feet. "Mom?" I called out. "I'm back!"

I turned the corner into the brightly lit living room. Mom was sprawled out on the fuzzy blue armchair next to a lamp. My breath caught, and for a moment I feared that something terrible had happened again. Then I saw her chest rise up and down slowly and I realized with relief that she had only fallen asleep.

Her arm hung over the edge of the armrest and she shifted restlessly. While sleeping, a permanent frown was imprinted on her face. I didn't like to see Mom like that. It occurred to me that I could dreamweave something to make her relax a little. I hadn't noticed how stressed out she had been lately.

I let the ball of energy fill me up until I felt the familiar tingling sensation run up and down my arms. Once I created the perfect dream (consisting of sunshine and rainbows, because, really, who doesn't like rainbows?), I realized that all my efforts would be futile without a dream sender to help me. Mom and I were alone in the house except for my cat, who had returned safely. I doubted Shelby was secretly a dream sender.

Disappointed, I let the tingling fade to numbness. On my own, I was useless. Would I always have to rely on someone else in order to help others?

With a sigh I headed to the hall closet and did the next best thing. I grabbed an extra blanket and draped it over my mom. "Sweet dreams," I whispered.

Chapter Thirteen

"It could be anywhere by now," I sighed, discouraged. Carson and I had just visited the grocery store in search of the infamous penny, with no luck. The cashiers had looked at us like we were crazy, even after I explained that it was a rare coin from my collection. They weren't about to let us look inside the cash register, either.

We walked along the streets of Fortune aimlessly. Fortune had been quiet ever since Mom returned from the hospital. I had seen no other signs of the nightmares the penny had unleashed, but that didn't mean they weren't here. It was the silence that scared me the most—the not knowing what was ahead, that made my skin prickle with foreboding.

Carson hadn't said anything for a while. I turned around halfway and then realized he was no longer next to me. "Carson?"

I glimpsed him behind me, talking with a small boy across the street. Carson knelt down and whispered something into the boy's ear. As I watched, Carson rummaged through his pocket and pulled out a brightly-colored lollipop. The boy smiled in delight as Carson presented it to him, and he raced off to show his mother his new prize.

Carson stood up unsteadily and headed back in my direction. When he reached my side, we resumed our pace. "You really like kids, don't you?" I commented, glancing toward Carson.

"Yes," he smiled briefly, seeming a bit lost in his memories. "I never had any."

We were silent again. It wasn't a stifling silence, but more of a comfortable one between companions. My mind wandered to all that was ahead for us, everything that had led us to be here. "Carson?"

He turned to look at me, giving me his full attention. "Yes, Audrey? What is it?"

"All of this—everything we've done—I can't help but think it might be all for nothing. What if I'm not ready?"

He regarded me solemnly, but not unkindly. "Audrey, you are so strong. I noticed that the moment I met you." His eyes met mine. "I will not lie; this town will soon be very much changed. The evil unleashed from the penny will not lie dormant forever. But I want you to know this: I will be with you every step of the way. You're not going into this alone." He paused for the slightest moment. "We *are* going to fix this."

I nodded, breathing in deeply. And I clung to hope.

It was several hours later when we caught sight of the penny. Carson and I had just decided to stop for the day when we turned a corner and came face to face with Mrs. Tweedy. "Oh!" she cried, nearly dropping her bulging purse. "Hello, Audrey!"

Carson stepped forward and smiled pleasantly. "Good afternoon, I'm Carson Gray."

Mrs. Tweedy seemed to notice him for the first time. "Well, hello there! Evangeline Tweedy. Simply lovely to meet you." She jabbered on, "I discovered the most terrible thing today! A tragedy, really. You'll never guess what happened." She didn't pause long enough for us to guess, even if we could. "I noticed it just this morning. I was looking for my pink fur coat and matching boa when I opened my closet door, and I just couldn't believe it! It was empty. I haven't the slightest idea how it happened, but somehow all of my wonderful outfits had disappeared! It was my worst nightmare!"

At that, Carson and I exchanged a glance. This sounded all too familiar. Mrs. Tweedy rambled on, unaware that we were no longer paying attention. "I had to borrow *this* from my sister," she gestured at the almost ordinary blue dress she was wearing. "It's just hideous." A look of disgust crossed her face.

Before Mrs. Tweedy could start talking again, Carson inquired, "Do you by any chance have any loose change?"

I looked at him in confusion but then realized what Carson was trying to do. "Oh, yes, I suppose I have some in here somewhere." Mrs. Tweedy dug through her purse and retrieved a small coin bag. She fumbled with the zipper and scooped out a handful of coins. "How much do you need?"

Carson was preparing to answer when Mrs. Tweedy accidently dropped her coins. Several quarters fell to the ground with small clinks. "Oh, dear me," she said, bending down quickly. As I crouched down to help her, I noticed a single penny had also fallen, rolling away on its side. I stood hastily and took a few quick steps after it. My head throbbed slightly, and I knew that this was the penny, that somehow it had come into the hands of Mrs. Tweedy. The words from her fortune cookie came back to me. *I will find myself a penny richer in the near future.* Her fortune had come true.

Before I could stop it, the penny rolled over to a group of people standing a few feet away. I lost sight of it among the many feet. I watched as a hand reached down and picked up something from the sidewalk. Leaving Carson and Mrs. Tweedy behind, I hurried over to where the penny had vanished, but the group of locals had already called out their goodbyes and dispersed, going their separate ways. I looked back and forth, frantically searching for that distinct gleam of metal in the light, but it was impossible to tell who now had possession of the penny.

Chapter Fourteen

So, she really *was* powerful! Jonathan hadn't fully believed it until he had seen it with his own eyes. He truly hadn't meant to eavesdrop, but now that he had he couldn't undo what he had discovered. Dreamweaving. That must have been the dangerous ability Sharpe was talking about. Jonathan couldn't really understand how it worked, but it wasn't particularly *bad,* was it?

He knew he had to return to Sharpe and tell him what had happened. After all, his uncle hadn't yet paid him a single dollar.

Before he could make any more decisions, dark, acrid smoke appeared in front of him, making Jonathan stop in his tracks. A faint scent of something that reminded Jonathan of burnt feathers arose in the air. Almost tangible tendrils curled and twisted around him and condensed into a hulking, dark mass.

Before he knew what had happened, Sharpe was standing in front of him imperiously.

"H–how did you do that?"

Sharpe considered for a moment. "It is time you know your family heritage. I am a Seer of Night. The ability to quickly travel to different places comes with that title."

"Seer of Night? So…you can see in the dark?"

Sharpe snorted. "You idiot! A Seer of Night is able to recognize darkness as it is and mold it to his will. A Seer of Night is capable of much more than any ordinary leader. Your father is not lucky enough to possess this trait but with a bit of learning, you could do well.

"Now then, what have you learned about the girl? Has she unknowingly revealed anything? Remember, this is your job."

Jonathan gulped. "Well, Audrey says she's a dreamweaver. Have you heard of that? I saw her practicing." He went on to explain as briefly as possible how she seemed to glow and an invisible wind arose around her every time she wove a dream.

Sharpe's face had grown a little pale. "Were you seen by anyone?" he interrogated forcefully.

"Uh, yeah. They saw me."

"They?"

"Audrey. She was with an older man. He was helping her, I think."

Sharpe's eyes bore into his own. "Who was this man?"

"I…think his name was Carson."

At the mention of the name, Sharpe stamped at the ground hard with his boot. Loose rocks trembled, and Jonathan could've sworn he felt the earth shake. "It is worse than I imagined," Sharpe growled between clenched teeth. "I did not think a mere girl would be able to do what she has already done so effectively and so soon. With that man, she will only grow more powerful."

Then Sharpe seemed to remember Jonathan was still there. He slapped a handful of bills into Jonathan's palm. "Your work is done for today. Continue to find out more from that girl and report back to me." As Jonathan turned to leave, he glanced down at the money still in his hand. His eyes widened. *Two hundred dollars* in twenty-dollar bills.

Chapter Fifteen

To the television newscaster, it was just another news report. "There's recently been a period of unrest for the citizens of Fortune, a tiny town over a hundred miles away from any large city." She paused to flash her picture-perfect smile. "We have received reports of unusual occurrences in this town before, but I believe this one tops them all."

Grainy, shaky footage began to play on the screen. It showed Fortune's Main Street lined with shops. A young girl about eight years old ran across the screen, looking absolutely hysterical. Her ragged breaths and panicked screeching for her mother could be heard on the video. The camera wobbled and suddenly swerved in the opposite direction away from the girl. A looming, furry creature roared an unrecognizable, throaty sound. It stood almost as high as the buildings around it. The camera was moving and shaking too intensely to identify the creature. It stood on its hind legs and bared a row of glistening, pointed teeth. It vaguely resembled a bear, but it was apparent that this creature was no bear. The creature ignored the people who stood unmoving in their fear, and it appeared to be intent on chasing one person only: the girl.

The video ended abruptly and the newscaster's face reappeared. "The animal in the footage has not yet been identified, but most scientists and researchers who have studied this footage have determined that this is no ordinary creature, resembling no specific species.

"Investigators on the scene have no answers as of yet. No trace of this mysterious creature has been found. However, several citizens of Fortune who wish to remain unnamed have their own ideas. They insist the creature is the child's manifested nightmare. We have been told that the people of Fortune have always been superstitious, but this incident begs the question: is this monster only an elaborate hoax, or is there some truth behind the witnesses' beliefs?"

Chapter Sixteen

I had started to meet with Carson every day, and I could really feel the difference in my abilities. It was much easier for me to dreamweave, and we did it as often as we could, but Carson didn't often have someone to send the dream to.

Now that Carson and I were working together, I always felt the heat and power within, no matter how deep it was inside me. It comforted me to know that I could do something useful, if only every so often.

Ever since the news report on Fortune was viewed on TV, we had more tourists than ever before. They all came to see "Bigfoot," as they had dubbed the monster, but I knew that they would never see it. It really *had* come from the girl's nightmares, but most people were dubious. I wondered how that fact had leaked out into the media.

Everyone did realize, though, that something was wrong in Fortune. The streets seemed darker than usual in the night, and by day everything was a little hazy, like the whole town was enveloped in a thin, gray cloud.

The penny I had found seemed to be causing it all. As far as I could tell, it kept changing hands, and no one was aware of what it was causing. It was like a disease—spreading around and, slowly but surely, affecting everyone. Yesterday Mr. Billings fell off the top of his ladder and had to be rushed to the hospital two hours away. The day before, the bakery had become infested with mice and had to be closed for the day to get rid of them.

Carson was worried about all of it. "When the nightmares are able to manifest into tangible things in broad daylight," he explained, "then you know it has gotten much worse."

We both knew that, but there wasn't much we could do about it. I had just begun trying to interrupt a dream in progress and change it, but it wasn't working as I wanted it to. For one thing, it was hard to tell if someone was already dreaming. Also, it involved untangling the mess of the knotted dream and adding in my own threads. It wasn't an easy thing to do. And even if I eventually perfected it, how much help would that be? I couldn't do much about the dreams manifesting outside of someone's mind—the nightmares that ravaged the city.

I wandered around Fortune aimlessly. Could I really have caused all this? I wished I could go back to that day and walk past that penny, never picking it up. I didn't know why my touch had unlocked a bit of the evil from Pandora's box, but I fervently wished that it hadn't. But there was no point; I couldn't undo what I had done.

I blinked several times in a row and found myself in the shopping square with the Fortune water fountain. The area was deserted, and shadows filled several shops' windows. Most of the tourists were probably lingering around the other end of Main Street, where their "Bigfoot" had been seen. Carson was probably somewhere around here too, but I didn't want to talk to him now.

The fountain bubbled, and a few drops of water flew at my face, making me laugh. The water didn't sparkle like it normally did, but it shone in the slight sunlight through the haze. The coins beneath the water almost covered the entire bottom of the fountain. Little ripples and splashes beckoned to me. It couldn't hurt, could it?

I fingered a quarter in my pocket and pulled it out, turning it over in my hands slowly. It winked at me in the light and I closed my eyes. I inhaled deeply and let the breath out my mouth. *I wish the nightmares were trapped back in Pandora's box again where they belong.*

I flicked the quarter into the fountain and watched it slap the water lightly and sink to the bottom. Droplets flew onto the side of the fountain, temporarily staining the white stone a darker color. I stared, mesmerized at the ripples growing and then fading, encircling the spot where the coin had fallen.

"Audrey?"

My breath caught and I spun around. For a moment I thought it was Carson, but Jonathan was standing next to me instead. "Sorry Jonathan," I told him, "I just can't practice now or try any more experiments. I'm just so, so tired of it all."

His gaze softened, and I thought perhaps he understood exactly what I meant. He had been dragged into all of this, after all. Or he had dragged himself.

"That wasn't what I was going to say."

"Oh." Why had he come to find me then?

"I thought you could use a break from dreamweaving. You let me see your favorite place. Now I want to show you *my* favorite place to be."

My eyes brightened. "Okay, you've got me intrigued. Let's go!"

Jonathan grinned and led me out of the shopping square and deeper into town. As we walked along the streets, we talked about anything and everything—except dreamweaving and nightmares. It truly felt good to ignore the problems for a while.

At one point I asked Jonathan about his job now that he no longer worked at the grocery store. "Oh," he hesitated for a moment. "My uncle hired me to be his assistant. He has his own lab in his house."

"That's so cool! Is he a scientist or something?"

"I guess you could call him that. He does a lot of…research, too."

I could tell he was uncomfortable, so I changed the subject and finally asked, "So where are we going, anyway?"

Jonathan brightened and grinned mischievously. "You'll see! I will give you fair warning, though. It's not like your favorite place. It's not even outdoors."

"Hmm. Well that narrows down the possibilities quite a bit," I commented.

We continued talking, and I got so caught up in our heated discussion about which was better— M&Ms or Skittles (I was all for Skittles, of course)— that I almost didn't follow when Jonathan made a sudden right off Main Street onto a smaller side street with more shops. They were fewer here and more widely spaced. We couldn't possibly be going to the car mechanic's store, could we?

We stopped in front of a small building with a faded blue awning and large front windows with frames that looked as if they had been recently painted. Inside I could see a window seat piled with a variety of pillows, and rows and rows of books. "The bookstore?"

"Hey, don't judge me yet," Jonathan smiled, raising his hands in mock defense. He pushed open the door with one hand and it creaked slightly. I looked around in surprise. It was larger than it appeared from the outside. Of course, I had been in the bookstore before—I had been in almost every store in Fortune—but it had been a while.

"Come on." Jonathan gestured for me to follow him, and he led me to a corner of the store. He grabbed a handful of books from a bookshelf against the wall while I watched in confusion. He set the books on a small table nearby and continued until he had bared half the shelf. I glanced around to make sure no one was glaring at us.

"Watch this."

I returned my gaze to the shelf and bent down so I could see the wall behind where the books had been.

Jonathan pushed against the wall carefully with his fingertips and I jumped slightly when it gave way. He removed a painted wooden board from the wall, and in its place was a rectangular space about a foot wide.

"Wow!" I exclaimed a bit too loudly. "A secret compartment!"

Jonathan laughed. "My mom works here on weekends, and she showed it to me. She said no one would mind if I kept things in it." He pulled out a large paperback book that barely fit in the hole. "I used to read this when I was little. It's still my favorite." He showed me the cover. It was *The Adventures of Huckleberry Finn*. "What about you? What was your favorite book when you were little?"

I considered. "I always liked *Tuck Everlasting*."

Jonathan nodded in appreciation and pointed at a bookcase a couple feet away. There were several copies of *Tuck Everlasting* on the top shelf. "Impressive," I commented. "It seems like you know this place well."

He replaced the wooden board and put the books back on the shelves. As we walked past a different room in the store, I heard voices and paused at the doorway. It sounded like someone was reciting poetry.

Jonathan stopped and looked back when he realized I was no longer following him. Noting my interest, he explained, "They're having a poetry reading. Want to go listen?"

I nodded and we entered, choosing seats in the back. There were probably twenty-five other people in the audience, mostly adults, but a few kids too. Standing in the front was a tall, slender woman with curly dark hair. A nametag on her sweater said her name was Callie.

"That's my mom," Jonathan whispered.

She began to speak and everyone quieted.

"Today I'm going to read a poem titled *The Bridge*, which is modeled after a type of poem called a Terza Rima.

Among the whispering trees there lies in shadows,
    The haunting memory of days that passed;
    A bridge stands silent over murky shallows.

The wooden beams, though ancient, always last,
But feet no longer cross this hidden way;
The bridge remains forgotten in the past.

Its beauty goes beyond what one can say —
Eternal power held in splintering wood;
Light fades and calls the ending of this day.

And night arose above the bridge that stood;
The orb revealed a glistening of hair,
And laughter filled the place that nothing could."

When she finished reading the poem, I felt numb. It reminded me of my own life. The penny I had picked up was my bridge to Carson and Jonathan. Even though it was so terrible, it connected me to the laughter and friendship I had received from them.

I marveled at how haunting and profound the poem was, and told Jonathan so. "Who wrote it?" I asked.

"*The Bridge*? My mom did."

"Really? She's a really good poet."

Jonathan laughed. "I guess you've found a new interest."

"What?"

"Poetry."

I thought about it. It was amazing how one poem could affect me so much. "I guess I have."

We left the room quietly when Jonathan said he wanted to show me something else. Once we were back in the main room of the bookstore Jonathan pushed open another door nearby, and I felt the chilly October air sweep across my face. "No fair!" I cried out playfully. "You said it wasn't going to be outdoors."

"Technically, it's not; we were inside. This is just extra," he countered. Behind the building was a little picnic area I'd never seen before. There were picnic benches scattered about, surrounded by hardy wildflowers still growing in patches. One huge, thick-limbed tree towered over a few other saplings, and hanging from it was a little wooden swing. I sat down on the seat of the swing and took all of it in. "This place is amazing," I spoke aloud. "I've lived here my whole life, and I never even knew it existed."

Suddenly, Jonathan strode toward me. "You are really going to regret getting on that swing," he teased, trying to sound serious.

"Oh, really?" I asked innocently. "Why is that?"

He laughed, grabbed the rope on either side of me, and pulled me back. When he released his grasp, I rocketed forward. I shrieked as the sky hurtled toward me.

It reminded me of swinging with Dad so long ago. This was different, yet the same. It was a good memory, and it made me happy to relive it again even though I had changed so much in the past ten years.

I laughed with pure joy and Jonathan joined in, too. The rough fibers of the rope against my fingertips and the sound of the wind rustling past my ears were enough to make anyone happy.

Jonathan gulped down another laugh and shouted over my continuing giggles, "Why are we laughing?"

"I have no idea!" I yelled back and burst into laughter again, solely because it felt good to do so. And because there was no reason not to.

My unladylike snickers turned into gasps

and, finally, sighs of contentment. For one blissful moment, there were no such things as monsters or nightmares. Everything was fine.

Chapter Seventeen

"It is most agreeable that you arrived when you did." Sharpe looked condescendingly down at Jonathan as though he was chastising him instead of paying him the closest thing to a complement he would ever give.

After a moment of wordlessly staring at each other, Sharpe seemed to give him silent permission to enter his lab.

Jonathan pushed open the double doors to the room, and Sharpe strode directly behind him. His uncle reached around him and flicked on the lights, illuminating all the equipment and automatically turning on the screens and monitors.

"I will teach you some of what I do. You must do exactly as I say, or it will not be helpful for either of us."

Jonathan did not like his tone but didn't comment on it.

Sharpe glided over to the counter with all the monitors against the wall and rested one twisted hand on a keyboard built into the countertop. "Sit," he told Jonathan, gesturing to a red swivel chair next to him.

"I am *not* a dog," Jonathan retorted. Was *this* the way his uncle treated his assistants?

Sharpe muttered some snide remark under his breath that Jonathan didn't catch. Then his uncle's attention turned to a tiny screen that was lit up with patches of bright red on a black background.

"What do those red areas mean, Uncle Sharpe?" Jonathan asked, indicating the spots on the device.

Sharpe growled in irritation at the name but finally answered. "This is the device I was telling you about that tracks darkness in the area. I constructed this myself." Here he swelled a little bit with pride. "The red marks on the map are the areas where darkness currently dwells."

Jonathan stared at the map in horror. The screen probably showed the whole town. And there was overall too much red on the map. Most of the town was covered in splotches of varying shades of red. Jonathan noticed some were fading and shifting slightly. The right side of the screen was what caught Jonathan's eye. It must've been the east side of town. One area was just a huge blood-red circle.

Jonathan pointed to the area and opened his mouth, but no words came out.

"Ah, yes, so you do have some brain cells after all."

Jonathan was too shocked to be indignant.

"*That* is where the penny is located at this time. Yes, you know what I am speaking of." Sharpe suddenly grew extremely angry. "It seems you neglected to inform me that the girl was no longer in possession of the coin," he seethed. "What I would very well like to know is why. That insignificant little trinket is the key to my success! Why, if I could just get my hands on it, then—" He broke off and glared at Jonathan. "What else have you been keeping from me?"

For the first time in his uncle's presence, Jonathan was frightened. "Nothing! I swear Unc—I mean, Sharpe, nothing! I didn't think to tell you that Audrey lost it."

Sharpe raised his eyebrows. "It never occurred to you that the penny injected with darkness could assist me?"

"What? No!"

His anger deflated and Sharpe's expression was again completely composed. Like nothing had happened, he said, "Very well. We shall return to our subject at hand."

It was eerie how volatile Sharpe's temper could be. One moment he was infuriated and the next, completely calm.

"Once I have the coin," Sharpe was saying, "it will be possible to use it to unleash the rest of the darkness that is still contained in Pandora's box. Of course, you can see that this map is not completely accurate and does not show many small details. This is unfortunate, because all it tells me is the person currently in possession of it is somewhere in East Fortune at this time.

"Now, it is obvious that I could simply travel to that location and follow the trail it leaves. In fact, I have tried that very thing. My senses for darkness are quite developed, after all. The most probable explanation for the unsatisfactory results is that no one citizen keeps it for long. However, I believe that my affinity for darkness shall bring me triumph in the end. I assume you have experienced the ability to sense darkness as well?"

Jonathan was taken aback. He *had* thought he felt the effects in the air when Audrey dreamwove, but the nightmares, or darkness, as his uncle called them, were completely different. Did he even *want* to be able to feel them? "No, at least, I don't think so," he responded.

Sharpe looked disappointed for a moment, but then his face glazed over in an expressionless mask. "That is most unfortunate. I was fairly certain you had the ability. Perhaps it has not shown itself fully yet. Although you should be able to sense it a bit whenever you are in my presence," Sharpe mused thoughtfully.

For some reason this did not surprise Jonathan a bit. His uncle seemed very interested in the darkness in Pandora's box—almost obsessed with it. It even seemed that Sharpe could appear in different places at will. For these reasons it wasn't surprising that some people could feel darkness when Sharpe was around. Sharpe *was* darkness. But the thing that disturbed Jonathan most was that with his uncle, he didn't really sense anything at all. He only felt a disturbing wariness.

Chapter Eighteen

"It's good to see you, Audrey." I was at the grocery store checkout buying bananas and some other fruit for Mom.

"Hi, Mrs. Jenkins," I greeted the lady behind the register.

As she scanned my purchases she glanced up at me, then looked back down. Then she did the same thing again. Finally I asked her, "Mrs. Jenkins, is there something wrong?"

"No, no," she said distractedly. "It's just…did you dye your hair?"

The question was so unexpected that I didn't answer for a moment. She knew my red hair was natural. Everyone did; it was one of the first things people noticed about me.

I grabbed a fistful of my hair and twisted it over my shoulder so I could see it better. My eyes bugged out. My hair was streaked with gold. My first thought was that I had rubbed against something, but when I held it between two fingers the color did not rub off. I remembered the few yellowish hairs I had had before, but it seemed that now whole strands had turned a soft gold. It was strikingly obvious, as if I had gotten it highlighted. I wondered how long it had been like that. What did it mean?

I told her that I hadn't dyed my hair, and all she said was, "Huh." Mrs. Jenkins handed me several bags and told me to have a nice day. As I walked out the doors, I caught sight of Mrs. Tweedy, who was visibly lacking her usual peacock feather hat.

"Hi, Mrs. Tweedy," I called out.

She turned and smiled slightly when she saw me. A worn-out expression on her face and dark bags under her eyes made her appear decades older than she really was. "Hello Audrey. I'm afraid I haven't been feeling very well of late. There must be a sickness or something going around. I just feel so sad and…tired." Then she brushed her own words aside with a flick of her hand. "Oh, don't mind me. I'm just lamenting about my problems again."

It was interesting that she could feel the effects of the nightmares, even if she didn't know what they were. That was probably how everyone else in town felt lately, too.

Suddenly, an ominous, dangerous feeling came over me, and something dank and cold swept past. "What was that?"

Mrs. Tweedy looked confused. "What?"

"Is there a storm coming in or something?" I looked up at the sky, but it was a dull blue. Not a cloud in sight.

"There was nothing in the forecast about a storm."

As soon as she spoke, a shrill, piercing alarm began to wail. Panic arose in the supermarket, and people came rushing outside only to stop and stand, transfixed. That was Fortune's emergency alarm. Something was very wrong.

"Smoke!" Mrs. Tweedy exclaimed. She was right. From this vantage point, we could see all of Fortune. And in the center of town, dark clouds of smoke billowed out and ascended into the air. I thought I saw a flicker of flames peek over the top of a building.

Without stopping to figure out what I was doing, I raced down the street and toward the center of town. While I sped in that direction, others were heading away from the fire. They were like a stampede of frightened animals—there was no stopping them.

Still, most of the people were gathered along the streets, either gaping at the commotion that ensued or standing still, frozen with shock. Why wasn't anyone doing anything? Fortune was too small for a fire station with many fire engines and full-time firefighters, but we did have a few volunteer firefighters and an old fire truck. So why was everyone panicking instead of taking action? Where were the firefighters?

My breath came in short gasps as I rounded a corner, bumping into a mother pushing a stroller in the opposite direction. What I saw made my heart pause mid-beat. The town hall had gone up in flames. But it wasn't any ordinary fire. The flames flared wildly in colors of blood red and orange—more vibrant than they would normally be. They engulfed almost the entire building, and all I could see of it was one of the front pillars. Fortunately, the other buildings in the plaza had not yet caught fire and were unharmed. For now.

Out of the corner of my eye, I saw the volunteer firefighters finally rush to the scene, but now even I knew it was hopeless. I had never seen a fire this bad before. There was something very different about this one.

I didn't have time to contemplate. I broke into action. "Is there anyone still inside?" I screamed over the roar of the flames and the terrified crowd that had gathered to watch, horrified. The flames seemed to shift and move on their own accord.

For a moment I feared my voice had been lost in the cacophony. Then someone wailed, "I don't know! It came so suddenly!"

"I can't find my son!"

"What's going on?"

My lungs filled with acrid smoke, and I began to cough violently. My eyes stung from being so close to the fire, and I blinked furiously. Then I felt a firm hand on my shoulder. "Are you all right, Audrey?"

I turned and saw a kind, concerned face looking at me. Carson.

"Yes, I'm fine. It's the nightmares, isn't it?"

Carson looked gravely at the burning town hall. "Yes, I'm afraid so. The fire is the nightmare of whoever holds the penny now."

He had confirmed what I had only guessed at. "We have to stop it. It's already too big for water to help much."

Suddenly, there was a blinding flash, and the flames seemed to grow even larger as they wrapped around the building in an impenetrable death grip.

***

Sharpe smiled in silent satisfaction. Everything was going exactly as planned. Certainly, there had been a couple of unexpected minor inconveniences, but he had been able to turn them to his favor.

He had felt the explosion of darkness the moment it had formed into a tangible substance. It was like a magnet, pulling him to its source. He had let darkness guide him as he disappeared into the inky ether. When he stepped out, he saw the grandeur and power of the darkness morphed into its full glory. The flames ate at the weak building easily. How convenient for Sharpe that it had chosen this moment to rise up. Soon, he would have that power. Surely then he would not feel like a weak man.

Sharpe raised his scarred hands over his head and through them burst a great fury of a substance neither quite solid nor completely a vapor. A shockwave split the ground and sent a deafening boom through the air. The people nearest him were knocked off their feet, but Sharpe still stood unmoving. He forced the substance into the flames, and with a smaller explosion the fire grew nearly twice as large. Sharpe smirked. Now he only needed to step back and let time do the rest. He glided into the shadows and disappeared.

***

We needed time. There wasn't enough of it in this chaos. "What do we do?" I yelled to Carson. Soon this fire would spread to other buildings. In a matter of hours, one nightmare could destroy the whole town.

Carson looked at me calmly but determinedly. "Audrey, it's time for you to dreamweave. That nightmare is powerful, but I believe you can do it."

I understood what he wanted me to do right away, but it seemed impossible. "You want me to unweave the nightmare and dreamweave it away? I can't. I'm not strong enough!" I protested, panicked. "I've never dreamwoven a dream that is outside of someone's mind before!"

Carson had to have noticed the raw panic and fear on my face, but somehow he stayed calm. "You can do it, Audrey. I know you can. You are stronger than you know."

"Audrey!" Jonathan ran up and stopped next to me, panting wildly and staring wide-eyed at the burning town hall. "What's going on?"

"It's the nightmares." I told him as quickly as I could what had happened and what I had to do. When I finished, Jonathan nodded. "I'll help you in any way I can," he assured me.

"As will I," Carson told me.

I took in a shaky breath. I tried but could not ignore the commotion around me. People were jostling each other in their panic to get away and falling over in an attempt to avoid the Fortune fountain, screaming. Someone bumped into me from behind and mere yards away the volunteers were still stubbornly carrying on. Dreamweaving was so conspicuous, but it was the only chance.

I let the little ball inside me go too quickly and it fizzed to life painfully underneath my skin. I cried out in pain but quickly regained control. Several people turned and stared at me, and I realized my skin was probably glowing. I turned away from the crowd and concentrated solely on the only important thing: the nightmare that was burning Fortune's most prominent building.

This spurred me into action. I began to think

of happiness. Mom rocking me to sleep at night. Dad singing completely off key. My clearing in the forest. My new friends Carson and Jonathan. Special birthdays and Shelby and chocolate fudge brownie ice cream and Fortune itself. I wove every happy memory together in my mind until I could think of no more.

"Now. Send it to me now!" I heard Carson's voice vaguely as though I was underwater. I felt his hand clasp mine firmly and the dream rushed from my arm into his, taking my energy with it. My arm fell limply at my side, and I watched as the power of the dream left Carson and he thrust it straight into the heart of the fire. For a moment, the flames parted and wavered ever so slightly. Then they returned to their original state and continued to burn. I let out the breath I hadn't realized I had been holding. "Again!" Carson urged me, but I caught a flash of something from the corner of my eye.

Suddenly the smell of singed feathers filled the air. I looked over just in time to see a crow perched on a stairway railing of a building nearby. I gasped. It was the crow I had seen before, the one that had watched me through my window, the one in my dreams. Its narrow eyes met mine, looking intently at me for a moment. Then it transformed. As its body distorted, a dark cloud enveloped the crow until only a dark, scarred man stood in its place. He paused there, a look of unwavering determination imprinted on his face, staring straight at us. Straight at me.

Jonathan had noticed him, too. His breath caught almost imperceptibly, and he backed up a step. I was too stunned to move.

"Hello, *Audrey*. And hello, Carson Gray," the man greeted us coldly. "Long time, no see."

I turned to Carson, astonished. "Carson, who is this man?"

Carson looked grim. "This is Viktor Sharpe. He caused quite a few problems for me back when he was searching for Pandora's box. He believes he can gain power through nightmares."

"That is because I can. And I will." Sharpe narrowed his eyes at me and frowned. "But it so happens that the girl is in my way. Therefore, I must interfere." Sharpe smirked at us. "Ah, yes. My nephew has proven himself quite useful." Then he turned to Jonathan and spoke roughly. "You know what to do. Grab her. She's coming with us."

Jonathan looked back and forth between me and Sharpe. What was going on? Jonathan was related to this man?

I narrowed my eyes at Jonathan when the realization hit me. Jonathan was not on our side. I had trusted him, and he had betrayed me. But still he hesitated.

Sharpe stared piercingly at Jonathan. "She is dangerous for this town and you know it. Grab her!"

Firm resolve hardened in Jonathan's eyes and he met Sharpe's eyes as the fire continued to burn. "I don't choose nightmares and I don't choose you. I'm sticking with Audrey and I don't want anything to do with you and your plan for world domination."

At his short speech my eyes widened in relief. This was the Jonathan I knew.

Disbelief was evident on Sharpe's face. "Why you—how dare you!"

"Audrey, dreamweave!" Carson was looking at me urgently, and I tore my gaze away from Sharpe. Carson stepped in front of me to shield me so I could concentrate. I tried, but it was useless. Suddenly, something dark shot out from Sharpe and straight toward Jonathan. He ducked and the air above him burst and crackled. "Hurry, Audrey!" he shouted at me.

I began to repeat what I had done the last time. I tried to let happiness fill me up, but it was harder than it had been before.

From the corner of my eye, a burst of color erupted from Carson and hit Sharpe in the chest. Sharpe doubled over, and then I could no longer see him.

"Keep going; he's gone!" Carson's voice had taken on a rasping sound, and his labored breaths sounded strange.

Jonathan was clearing space around us so we could get closer to the fire. "Stand back," he ordered the bystanders. "We're trying to help."

I dreamwove again and again, each time growing a little more tired. When I transferred to Carson, the energy jumped through the space between us and violently left him. Finally I stopped. Carson was leaning heavily against a lamppost on the sidewalk. "It's not working!" I shouted. "It's not enough."

The flames were burning dangerously close to the building next to the town hall. I could barely see anything through the smoke and began to cough, a hacking sound that tore at my throat. I had made a small dent in the fire, but it wasn't enough.

I turned away, and that was when it caught my eye. A new burst of flames had flared up. The fire had spread. My eyes widened. "Guys, come here!"

Jonathan hurried over to me, and Carson followed close behind. How had I not noticed it before? Now not only the town hall was burning. So was the Fortune fountain.

The water boiled and bubbled as the intense flames danced on the surface. It was a surreal scene that was almost too bright to look at. Sparks ran up the body of the horse statue and burst from the mouth of the statue. It was at that moment that I realized that this horse was no unicorn—it was a dragon.

"Look!" Jonathan cried, his finger pointing up at the mouth of the horse. Something glinted in the light of the great inferno. It was a penny. *The* penny. Clenched in the teeth of the horse sculpture.

"Is that—" Jonathan started, and I nodded in confirmation. It was unmistakable. I could feel the nightmares that formed around it.

The penny dislodged itself from the statue and tumbled downward, coming to a stop at our feet. Once again, it rested tails side up. The penny hissed and crackled, spitting sparks into the air. Jonathan bent down. "Don't touch it!" Carson and I yelled at the same time. Jonathan abruptly pulled back his outstretched arm and straightened. "What do we do?"

"If the penny is destroyed, the nightmares it unleashed will return to Pandora's box," Carson said slowly. Then he looked straight at me and I knew what I had to do. We couldn't touch the penny with our bodies, but there was something else that might work.

"Ah, so you have found what I, too, have been seeking," a voice sneered. I looked up, alarmed. It was Sharpe. He had returned.

"Don't do this, Sharpe," Carson said, and it almost sounded as if Carson were pleading with him. "It won't work. The nightmares will use you. They won't comply with what you want them to do for you."

"Silence! I shall not listen to your ridiculous claims. I may do what I wish. They shall obey me. And now, I believe you have something that is mine."

We all stood firm around the penny. Electricity sizzled around Sharpe and he looked at us calculatingly. Then something within him snapped. The thick cloud of nightmares that surrounded him shaped into a ball of darkness. Before I could grasp what was happening, he hurtled it straight at me.

Carson jumped in front of me and was hit with the full force of it. The ball of darkness exploded into tiny shards that pierced his skin without leaving a mark. He crumpled to the ground and did not move.

"Carson!" I screamed and fell onto my knees next to him, sobbing. His eyes were still open, and he moved them toward me slowly. His forehead creased in pain, but he did not cry out. "Audrey..." he whispered weakly. "You must...destroy the penny. It's the...only way."

"I can't!" I protested. "Not with you hurt. I can only gather my power, not send it into the penny!"

"Please..." his voice faded and he closed his eyes.

"Carson!" I screamed again, but he was still breathing shallowly.

"Audrey, hurry!" Jonathan shouted. He was trying to wrestle Sharpe away, but Sharpe merely deflected him with bursts of darkness. What could only be described as light flooded through me. It was not a dream, but rather the very real essence of everything that was good. It poured from my fingertips like a flow of golden water. Then it entered the penny. For a moment the penny only glowed, growing brighter and brighter.

A shrill, tinny screech resounded through the air. It became deafening, and I clapped my hands over my ears. Jonathan did the same, but Sharpe stared at me incredulously. Something like fear flickered in his eyes, and he disappeared in a cloud of black.

I turned back to the penny, ears still covered. As I watched, a crack formed on the surface, and it broke apart, shattering into a pile of dust.

Everything was quiet. Jonathan and I looked at each other. The only sound was the murmuring of the crowd that I had forgotten was there. A wind blew up and took the dust with it, and then nothing remained of the penny.

Chapter Nineteen

Jonathan and I knelt over Carson. Tears welled up in my eyes and threatened to spill over. I thought of my father in the hospital the night he died. Carson had reminded me of him so much.

Carson's eyelids fluttered and then opened fully. He smiled when he saw me. "I am so proud of you," he whispered. "You did it."

I allowed myself one moment to smile briefly. I guessed I had. "You saved me."

"Of course. Always." Carson smiled softly. Then he saddened. "There's something I should tell you."

"Don't worry, just rest," I told him quickly, but he didn't listen.

"I used to put pennies on the ground for people to find," he began quietly. "It was a way to make people happy. I placed them heads up. Always heads up." He took in a shaky breath and his expression changed to one of remorse. "Except for one time. There was one time I wasn't careful. One time when I wasn't watching. I dropped a penny. And it landed on the wrong side."

A shiver went down my spine. "What are you saying?"

He looked straight into my eyes. His eyes were full of deep sorrow. "I think the penny I dropped was the one you picked up."

I looked at him in shock. Was it true? I had thought it was someone cruel, like Sharpe, who left the penny lying there, not Carson, the kindest person I knew. But the sadness in his eyes told me it had to be true.

"I didn't notice it was gone until later. By then it was too late."

I couldn't be angry with him. He hadn't meant to leave that penny for me to find. After all, I had chosen to pick it up. "It's all right," I assured him. "I forgive you."

He looked at me in surprise and then smiled, the skin around his mouth creasing slightly. "You are an unusual girl, Audrey. That is a good thing." He paused for a moment. "Keep dreamweaving. I think that's what you're meant to do."

Carson reached out and grasped my hand in his lightly. I felt raw power flow into me, tingling and warm. After a moment, it stopped, and Carson's hand fell limply at his side. A smile was still on his face when he closed his eyes for the last time.

✳✳✳

Although the people of Fortune didn't truly understand what we had done, they were extremely grateful. When I had turned the penny to dust, the fire had faded until it was no more than a few flickering flames. The people were able to then contain it and put it out completely.

The town hall would have to be almost

completely rebuilt, but it was not a total loss as most people had feared. The townspeople were relieved that none of the other buildings had been harmed.

Miraculously, the Fortune fountain was, for the most part, unscathed. Other than the white stone that had been scorched in areas, it was intact and undamaged.

Jonathan and I were considered heroes. Through all the interviews and pictures, though, I felt numb. The loss of Carson was a terrible blow. Even Jonathan was somber, and he hadn't known him as well as I had.

***

I walked along the streets of Fortune once again. Much had changed. We citizens had gotten together and fixed up the town. We put a new coat of paint on all the buildings, made new store signs, and even began repairing the town hall. It was a slow process, but everyone helped.

A young boy ran along the sidewalk clutching a bright yellow kite. A strong breeze blew past and the boy rushed to an open field before it died down.

The air felt bitter against my face, and my nose was red from the cold. I blew on my hands to keep them warm.

I hadn't seen any sign of the nightmares since I had banished them to Pandora's box. But I knew they weren't gone forever. People like Sharpe were searching for the box, and it would only be a matter of time before another penny landed on tails and someone with a powerful ability picked it up. It really was only the beginning.

Neither Jonathan nor I had seen any more of Sharpe either. Jonathan had told me that Sharpe was his uncle. Sharpe had escaped Fortune, but Jonathan had a feeling that he would return eventually.

As I walked past the bookstore (which now had a new brighter blue awning), Jonathan came out and fell into step beside me. I didn't say anything for a moment.

"A penny for your thoughts," Jonathan teased.

I laughed softly. "Ugh. I never want to hear that saying again."

He grinned. "I guess not." We were silent for a minute.

"I've just been thinking how much things have changed, I guess." I looked out in the distance at the rolling plains and forever-changing sky. A month ago I never would have thought I'd be where I was now. I was a dreamweaver. I had found a place in my town. I had been able to send a dream once, but I didn't know how I could go on without Carson Gray.

Unknowingly, we had wandered to the plaza. I turned away from the broken form of the town hall and focused my gaze on the Fortune fountain. I remembered Carson's words: *You can find me here. Always here.* But I would no longer be able to see him at the fountain. It was hard to think about that. I circled the fountain slowly, and Jonathan hung back without a word.

When I reached the spot where we had sat and spoken, I saw something lying on the rim. It was a shiny, new penny. And it was facing heads up. I tilted my head toward the sky above in wonder. Maybe I wasn't as alone as I thought. Droplets of water sprinkled my face, and I smiled.

Acknowledgments

Wow, I wrote a book! So many authors say it never would have been possible for them without all the help they received along the way, and now I know how true that is. Thanks to everyone who helped me weave this dream of mine into reality:

First and foremost, thanks to Catie, who introduced me to NaNoWriMo and had the idea for the library to start this contest in the first place. To everyone else in Parker's Teen Library Council (we'll always be Tabbers at heart), for applauding every time and adding a little bit of healthy chaos to my life.

To the staff at Parker library, especially Peggy H. and Gail. You encouraged me and cheered me on every step of the way and somehow managed to keep the results of the contest secret until the right time.

To my cover designers, Shantana Judkins and Susan O'Brien. Thank you for bringing Audrey to life on that breathtaking cover. To Peggy Peterson, my amazing editor, for the long phone conversations and for never settling for "good enough." Thanks to BookCrafters for making the whole publication process so much easier than I imagined.

Thanks to Rebecca, who read the first draft when everything was different and liked it anyway. To my writing camp buddies, Megan and Holly, who didn't hesitate when I asked them to read the summary and give their feedback, and to Nanci Marr, who made it even better.

I'm so grateful to the folks at NaNoWriMo. You made me write more in thirty days than I had ever before.

To everyone and everything that inspired me, including the song "Unwritten," by Natasha Bedingfield, and the man at Chick-fil-A, who reminded me of Carson.

And finally, a huge thank-you to my family. Thank you for reading my story too many times to count and never running out of answers to my questions. Mom and Dad—thank you for letting me talk about Audrey as if she was a real person. My brothers, David, Brian and Adam—thanks for being patient when I wouldn't let you read the story yet. Yes, I left in the cat.

Lauren Hallstrom was 15 when she wrote *Dreamweaver* during NaNoWriMo, a nationwide challenge to write a novel in 30 days. Her novel won Douglas County Libraries' NaNoWriMo contest and was chosen to be sponsored for publication.

Lauren lives in Parker, Colorado with her parents, three younger brothers, and a hyper cat. When she's not homeschooling or volunteering at the library, she spends her time reading voraciously, writing poetry, and dreaming up new stories.

To learn more about National Novel Writing Month, visit www.nanowrimo.org.